GHOST of a GUNFIGHTER

Also by Wayne C. Lee
in Large Print:

Law of the Lawless
Prairie Vengeance
Trail of the Skulls
Warpath West
Gun Country

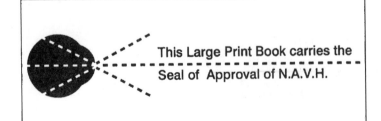

GHOST of a GUNFIGHTER

Wayne C. Lee

Published in 2005 by arrangement with Golden West Literary Agency.

Wheeler Large Print Western.

The text of this Large Print edition is unabridged.
Other aspects of the book may vary from the original edition.

Set in 16 pt. Plantin by Ramona Watson.

Printed in the United States on permanent paper.

Library of Congress Cataloging-in-Publication Data

Lee, Wayne C.
      Ghost of a gunfighter / by Wayne C. Lee.
          p. cm. — (Wheeler publishing large print westerns)
      ISBN 1-59722-017-5 (lg. print : sc : alk. paper)
          1. Large type books.   I. Title.   II. Thorndike Press large
print Western series.
      PS3523.E34457G48 2005
          813′.54—dc22   2005008688

GHOST of a GUNFIGHTER

As the Founder/CEO of NAVH, the only national health agency solely devoted to those who, although not totally blind, have an eye disease which could lead to serious visual impairment, I am pleased to recognize Thorndike Press* as one of the leading publishers in the large print field.

Founded in 1954 in San Francisco to prepare large print textbooks for partially seeing children, NAVH became the pioneer and standard setting agency in the preparation of large type.

Today, those publishers who meet our standards carry the prestigious "Seal of Approval" indicating high quality large print. We are delighted that Thorndike Press is one of the publishers whose titles meet these standards. We are also pleased to recognize the significant contribution Thorndike Press is making in this important and growing field.

Lorraine H. Marchi, L.H.D.
Founder/CEO
NAVH

* Thorndike Press encompasses the following imprints: Thorndike, Wheeler, Walker and Large Print Press.

Chapter 1

Dave Paxton rode toward Monotony with all the wariness born of years of experience in facing unknown enemies. He had ridden over three hundred and fifty miles, from Fort Reno in Oklahoma Territory to southwestern Nebraska, stopping only when his horse had to rest and graze. The one break in that long trek had been at Fort Hays in Kansas where he'd sent a telegram to Mark Horn, the lawyer in Omaha, telling him he was on his way to Monotony and would meet him there.

His horse lifted his head, catching a scent that had escaped Paxton. That could only mean water, probably Cottonwood Creek. They had put a lot of dry miles behind them, and it was a hot day for September.

Topping the long grassy knoll that overlooked the creek, he let his horse break into a long trot down to the water. His eyes ran up and down the valley, but he saw no signs of current habitation. He'd have to find someone to ask where Joshua Greer's place was, and he might have to ride into Monotony to do that but according to Roy's letter, that could be dangerous. He dug a crumpled letter from his pocket and while his horse sucked water from the creek, he read it for the tenth time.

September 1, 1878

Dear Dave,

I hope you get this in time. Uncle Josh was killed three days ago. Shot in the back down by the spring. Nobody knows who did it. Elias Norrid wants this spring for his Circle N. He may have done it himself or hired a killer. Lawyer Horn says you and Gary are to inherit this place. I'll stay here till you come. Hurry! I think they'll kill me too, if I stay very long. I can't fight them but you can. They know about you because Uncle Josh talked about his gunfighting nephew. So be careful. You'll be a marked man when you come. Uncle Josh had enemies other than Norrid and Tidrow of the Circle N. I'll tell you about that when you get here. Come as soon as you can. If I'm not here when you come, the stump will be our mailbox.

Roy

As he had done every time he read the letter, he stared at it, trying to read between the lines. Who were Josh's other enemies? There was something that Roy wasn't telling him. Why didn't he tell him? That in itself was a mystery.

While his horse rested and drank again, he studied the valley. Two dugouts were in sight, but both had obviously been abandoned some time ago. Plots of sod along the creek had been turned over but were growing high with weeds now. It would take years for grass to reclaim that ground.

Chalk bluffs rose from the meadow a hundred to two hundred yards beyond the opposite bank of the creek. In some areas, the bluffs had crumbled away and grassy slopes had taken their place, but nowhere did he see any sign of human life.

It was strange country to Paxton. Born in Illinois and brought up in eastern Kansas by his foster parents, John and Elisa Greer, he had grown up in a land of trees and fields. This land in southwestern Nebraska was devoid of trees except along the creeks, and even there, the trees were scattered or in small groves. There were no fields, only miles of prairie grass.

Paxton had been serving as civilian scout for the army at Fort Reno when he received the letter from the lawyer, Mark Horn, saying that Joshua Greer was dead. Paxton and his brother, Gary, were to inherit Joshua's land on Cottonwood Creek providing they appeared together in Monotony before October 4 to claim the inheritance. Paxton knew that was Joshua's way of making sure that the two brothers got together again.

Roy's letter had arrived the next day. That was the day that Paxton resigned as army scout and headed north. There was much about Roy's letter that puzzled him, but he did understand his mention of the mailbox.

Roy was five years older than Paxton, but they had played a lot together as Paxton grew up. They had secret places where they hid notes to each other. Apparently, Roy intended to leave a letter for Paxton in case he got too scared to stay on the land.

One thing puzzled Paxton more than anything else. Why was Roy staying at all if there was danger that he might be killed? Roy had never struck Paxton as the kind who would risk danger if he could avoid it. And surely he could avoid this danger; all he'd have to do was leave. Nobody was going to steal the land before Paxton and

Gary got there. Roy must have a compelling reason for staying. That and the mystery about Joshua's other enemies had put spurs to Paxton in his ride to Nebraska.

Having satisfied his thirst, Paxton's horse backed out of the creek and began nibbling at the grass along the bank. Paxton touched his flanks and guided him downstream. There was a road of sorts there that surely led to the town of Monotony.

He moved from the almost treeless meadows along the banks of the creek into a big grove of cottonwood trees. From there, he caught a glimpse of the town. A road wound through box elder, ash trees and scatterings of cottonwoods, which grew throughout the valley, some reaching as high as sixty feet tall.

Beyond the grove, the valley widened, and the bluffs faded into long slopes. The town was at the base of the left-hand slope, and most of the buildings were on the first and second benches above the creek bank level. It wasn't much of a town, perhaps twenty or twenty-five buildings in all.

Just before passing the last of the trees, a man leaped into his path from behind a big cottonwood. He had a gun centered on Paxton.

"Stop right where you are or you're dead!" the man shouted.

Paxton didn't wait to be told twice. "I'm stopped," he said, eyeing the man. "What's the idea?"

The man was small, younger than Paxton, not much more than twenty. He had dark hair and eyes, and right now, he was more scared than Paxton. A scared man holding a gun was as dangerous as an aggravated rattlesnake.

"You can't kill my boss then ride around like you owned the world," the man said, excitement and fear cracking his voice.

"I haven't been here long enough to kill anybody," Paxton said patiently. "I just came from Fort Reno in Oklahoma Territory."

The man looked at the weary horse, then back at Paxton. He shook his head. "You ain't never left the country."

"Who am I supposed to have killed?"

"My boss," the man repeated. "Roy Greer."

Paxton stiffened, jolted as if he'd been hit with a club. "When was Roy Greer killed?" he asked when he could control his voice.

"Three days ago. Maybe you thought nobody would recognize you if you showed up again. But I know you, and you're going to pay for what you done."

"Hold on!" Paxton exclaimed, sensing that he was only a breath away from eternity. "You've got me mixed up with someone else. My name is Dave Paxton."

The man frowned, easing his finger off the trigger. "Roy talked about a Dave Paxton." He stepped closer and peered intently into Paxton's face, his gun never wavering. Finally he stepped back, shaking his head in bewilderment. "You ain't the man I thought you was," he said.

"Don't I get a better explanation than that?" Paxton demanded.

The man let his gun sag. "I'm Jeff Rooker. My pa had a homestead up the creek till somebody killed him. I figure it was the Circle N. I got a job with Joshua Greer up at the spring. After he was killed, I stayed on with Roy. Roy was killed by a total stranger. I was in the barn when he rode in, and I saw him clear. You look enough like him to be his twin brother."

"Why would a stranger kill Roy?"

"I figure he was hired to do it. A lot of people wanted us off that spring, especially Elias Norrid and Sam Tidrow. Tidrow runs the Circle N for Norrid. They wanted to water their cows there. But it

13

could have been some other reason."

Paxton frowned. "What makes you say that?"

"Roy was scared, but it wasn't all because of the Circle N. There were strange riders at night and holes dug all around the spring. I told Roy we ought to leave, but he wouldn't. He even sent me on errands while he stayed there alone. I was just ready to leave for town to buy some grub the day that gunman rode in and shot him."

"Do you know the man's name?"

"I heard somebody say there was a stranger in town named Kucek. Most people figure he was the killer." He shook his head. "You sure do look like him."

The sound of a galloping horse turned both men toward town. A rider was coming up the river road from town. Rooker stepped back toward the trees. "Norrid runs that town. If you're a friend of the Greers, you'd better stay out of there."

Paxton stared at the spot where Rooker had vanished among the trees. He certainly did consider himself a friend of the Greers. After all, the Greers had given him a home after he was orphaned when he was four. Roy Greer had seemed more like a brother to him than his real brother who had been adopted by the Wirths. Paxton hadn't seen his real brother, Gary Wirth, since he was two.

Town probably wasn't the place for him to go, but he had more unanswered questions now than he'd had before he'd been stopped by Jeff Rooker. Somebody in town ought to have some answers. The lawyer, Mark Horn, should be there. Horn had said he had an office in Monotony before he moved to Omaha.

The approaching rider reined off the road before Paxton met him, and Paxton turned his attention to the town. Riding down the street between the first two buildings, the livery stable on one side and a feed store on the other, he passed the pool hall with a sign over a door down the alley near the rear of the building that said, "Deputy Sheriff."

The general store was next, and he dismounted in front of it. Two men and a woman came out of the store. They stopped as if they'd been stung with a whip and stared at Paxton. The woman gasped, and the men hurried her away down the street past the bank.

He walked into the store, quickly locating the overweight storekeeper behind the counter. The man was staring at him as if he were looking at a ghost.

"What do you want?" the man finally asked.

"Where can I find the man who killed Roy Greer?" Paxton asked bluntly.

The man's face blanched and he backed against the shelf behind him. "Why are you picking on me?" he whined. "I never did you any harm."

Paxton frowned. "I'm not the man who killed him if that's what you're thinking."

The man laughed shakily. "Of course, you ain't. Nobody said you were."

"You don't know where he is?"

The man shook his head so vigorously that Paxton thought it would snap off. "I never saw him in my life."

Paxton walked outside. He wouldn't learn anything there. The man was scared out of his wits. A blacksmith shop was directly across from the store, which meant there were farmers in the country. Most ranchers did their own blacksmithing, but farmers depended on the town smithy. He crossed to the shop, his boots kicking up the dust.

The light was dim inside, but the man wielding the hammer at the anvil stopped work when he came in. Paxton repeated his question and got an answer laced with fear. Paxton realized that whoever had killed Roy Greer had been in town long enough to intimidate every man here, even if nobody knew him well enough to recognize that Paxton wasn't the same man.

"Is there a lawyer named Horn in town?" Paxton asked.

"Was," the smithy said. "Moved away fast right after Josh Greer was killed. His office is over yonder just like he left it."

Paxton nodded and went back outside. A side street cut across the main street, and beyond the intersection was a bank and a drug store. Next door to the bank was a little building that had a sign painted on the window, "Mark Horn, Attorney at Law."

Paxton angled across the street to the lawyer's office, noting the big hotel just down the road. Across from the hotel was a small millinery shop, and a church sat beyond it, almost at the end of the street.

The lawyer's office was locked. Paxton looked through the window but curtains blocked his view of anything inside. Mark Horn mustn't have returned from Omaha yet.

Turning back, he saw that there were several people on the porch of the general store now, and all were watching him. His intuition warned him that this could mean trouble. He had to face them, however, because his horse was racked in front of the store.

He started toward the horse, moving in front of the bank and crossing the intersection to the porch of the general store. He saw a boy break away from the crowd and dash along the walk in front of the pool hall, then duck down the alley. Paxton remembered the Deputy Sheriff sign above the door at the back of the pool hall.

As Paxton crossed the porch of the store, the people fell back reluctantly. There were more than a dozen on the porch now, and their numbers bolstered sagging sparks of courage. Paxton could feel the hatred in the crowd. He had faced hatred before, but he'd always been looking into the faces of known enemies. How could these people be his enemies? He had never seen them before, and they had never seen him.

As Paxton stepped off the porch to his horse, the crowd surged forward, led by the huge storekeeper. Flipping the reins off the hitchrack, he wheeled to face the people on the porch, much as he would keep his face to a dog intent on nipping his heels. They wouldn't do anything as long as he faced them.

The boy came racing back with a short,

rather heavyset man in tow. Paxton saw the star sagging from the man's shirt front. He didn't want a confrontation with the law. He had come here to find and possibly kill a man, but he wanted to know he had the right man. He was sure he wasn't in this crowd.

"You're under arrest," the deputy shouted as he neared Paxton. He had his gun in his hand.

"What for?" Paxton demanded.

"For killing Roy Greer," the deputy puffed. "Didn't you think we'd all recognize you?"

"You're cornering the wrong wolf, deputy. I just got here."

"Try telling that to a jury of these people," the deputy said, waving his arm at the crowd.

As the officer reached for Paxton, Paxton took a backward step. That seemed to be a signal to those watching. They surged off the porch like water from an upset bucket and swarmed over him.

Paxton stayed on his feet by backing against his horse. He wondered if he would be killed right here, stamped to death by this miniature mob. If he wasn't, he'd be dragged off to jail. Considering the mood of this town, that would probably only postpone the inevitable.

Chapter 2

Backed against the shoulder of his horse, Paxton tried to push the people away. Perhaps if he could talk calmly with the deputy, he could make him believe he wasn't Roy Greer's killer.

The deputy was shoved out of the mob by the men fighting to get close enough to throw a punch at Paxton. A couple of women stood on the porch and cheered the men on.

From the corner of the porch, the deputy lifted his gun and fired it in the air. The fighting stopped, suspended as if every muscle had been paralyzed.

"You kill-crazy idiots!" the deputy shouted. "Get back and let me have that prisoner. He gets a trial even if we know he's guilty."

"Why waste money on a trial?" one man demanded. "Hanging is too good for him."

Paxton picked out the speaker and was surprised at his garb. Most of those who had rushed him were storekeepers or farmers. But this man wore the boots and Levi's of a ranch hand. According to what Rooker had said, the ranchers had wanted Roy Greer off that spring. Why would they want to hang the man now who supposedly had killed Roy?

There was more driving these people than just fear of a killer, Paxton decided as the deputy pushed him through the crowd onto the board sidewalk. The crowd followed a few feet behind as the deputy guided Paxton past the pool hall and down the alley between the pool hall and the feed store.

Paxton could see now that there were two side doors back here. The one opening into the room at the rear of the pool hall had the sign over it that said it belonged to the deputy sheriff, Tug Buskey. Across the narrow alley, the door opening into the back of the feed store led into a room with a barred window. That must be Monotony's jail. Paxton was sure he'd soon find out.

Buskey headed directly for the door into the rear of the feed store. Taking a key from his pocket, he unlocked the door and shoved Paxton inside.

"Cool your heels in there till the judge comes around," Buskey said.

"He's not liable to come here," Paxton retorted.

"When he gets to the county seat, I'll take you up there," the deputy said.

"They'll drag me out and hang me before that."

Buskey shook his head. "They won't get into that jail. It may not look like much, but it's sturdy."

The deputy turned and walked across the narrow alley and into his office. Paxton guessed that there was a partition door between Buskey's office and the pool hall. If that was like other pool halls he'd seen, there'd be a bar at one end. Buskey probably spent his leisure time at that bar. In Monotony, his leisure time must add up to a big percent of his waking hours.

Buskey had hardly disappeared when some of the more vociferous members of the mob who had attacked Paxton in front of the store began screaming at him.

"No murderer is going to live in this town," one yelled.

From the safety of his cell, Paxton had a chance to look over those who were yelling. There was a small barred opening in the door, but it was from the window that opened onto the alley that he got the best look. Parallel bars were two inches apart and gave him a good view. There was another door, permanently locked, in the partition between the cell and the feed store.

The one doing the loudest yelling in the alley was the man dressed in Levi's and boots. He certainly was no farmer or storekeeper. He would look at home only on a horse. But if he was one of the ranch hands, why was he in this mob? It wasn't likely that Roy Greer had been a personal friend.

It was ironic, Paxton thought, that the people out there howling for his blood right now would likely be the very ones who would be siding with him if they knew who he was and why he had come to Monotony. But until he knew more about the situation, he wasn't going to identify himself as the man who had come to even the score with the murderer of Joshua Greer. Now his vengeance would expand to include Roy Greer's killer too.

He stood close to the window and watched the people in the alley. Only four men and a boy were still out there. Standing close to the cowboy was a man he hadn't seen in front of the store. He didn't say much, just watched, his beady black eyes studying Paxton through the bars. He was an older man with white hair and a white mustache. His white eyebrows

23

contrasted sharply with the black eyes that looked as if they could pierce through steel. He wore a business suit but had a wide-rimmed gray hat.

The other two men looked like riffraff to Paxton, and he ignored them. The cowboy was the loudest yeller of the bunch. The boy, about ten, did his share of yelling too, looking to the old man for approval.

"Al Zamora is gathering up some more men," the cowboy yelled at Paxton. "When they get here, we're going to drag you out of there and string you up."

Paxton didn't honor the threat with any reply. He'd remember the cowboy and the old man if he ever got out of this. There was little doubt in his mind that the cowboy wasn't just bragging when he said they'd break him out of the jail and hang him. That little mob had demonstrated its willingness to kill out in front of the store. If the deputy hadn't fired his gun in the air, those men would have beaten him to death right there.

He thought of the deputy who had conveniently disappeared now. If he was at the bar in the pool hall, he couldn't help hearing the yelling in the alley. A good lawman would send everybody home.

When Buskey had rescued Paxton from

the little mob out by the store, he had appeared to be a real lawman, but Paxton wasn't sure about him now. He looked physically strong enough to manhandle any one of those outside the jail, but he didn't strike Paxton as one who would risk his life in pursuit of his duty.

Paxton tired of watching the men. They weren't going to do anything until they got reinforcements. The cowboy had practically admitted as much. Paxton wondered what had happened to the others who had helped the cowboy out in front of the store. All but the two loafers had disappeared. The old man had joined the cowboy only after Paxton was in jail. Maybe he had come out of curiosity but Paxton doubted that. He seemed intently interested in what was going on.

The old man was the first to leave, and the two loafers soon followed. Finally, with a parting threat, the cowboy went back to the front of the store. Only the boy stayed, curiosity and excitement gleaming in his face.

Paxton moved back to the barred window. "Who was that cowboy, sonny?" he asked.

The boy jumped when he spoke, and Paxton thought he was going to run. Then he apparently thought better of it since Paxton was behind bars. He came a step closer to the window.

"Don't make no difference to you, mister," he said, taking malicious pleasure in the situation. "They're going to hang you."

"I'd like to know who's doing it," Paxton said.

"You ought to know everybody from the other time you was here."

"This is my first time here, and I don't know anybody."

The boy frowned. "You can stick to that story till you're blue in the face. You ain't fooling nobody, especially that cowboy, Vic Ortis. You've got to remember him."

Paxton shook his head. "I don't know the old man either."

"Old Elias Norrid?" the boy exclaimed. "He's the banker."

"Do you know a man named Gary Wirth?"

The boy stared. "Do you aim to kill him? Or is he supposed to get you out of this fix?"

"Neither one," Paxton said. "I was to meet him here."

The boy moved a step closer, doubt showing clearly in his face. "Did you get a whack on the head and forget everything you ever knew? You really don't remember Mr. Norrid or Vic Ortis, do you?"

"I said I didn't," Paxton said patiently. "Do you know Gary Wirth?"

"I've heard the name," the boy said. "He was in town asking about a man named Paxton. I don't know where he went."

Paxton decided against telling the boy who he was. If Norrid knew who he was, Paxton might be in worse trouble, if that was possible. One thing was certain. His real brother, Gary Wirth, was here in town, or at least, he had been.

The boy stared at Paxton for another minute then turned and ran back to the street. Paxton went to the cot along the wall and sat down, scowling at the way things were going. It wasn't in his nature to sit back and wait for trouble to overwhelm him.

His mind raced back over the year, trying to put together a picture for which he had only scattered pieces. He had been four and his brother, Gary, had been two when they had been orphaned. John Greer and his wife had taken in Dave Paxton but had never adopted him so he had retained his real name. But the Greers were his family as much as if he'd been born a

27

Greer. Joshua Greer, who had preempted the land with the spring on Cottonwood Creek, was like a blood uncle to him.

Gary had been adopted by Frank Wirth and his wife, and he had taken their name. They had moved to Texas and Paxton, living in eastern Kansas, had not seen his brother since then. That had been twenty-two years ago. Gary would be twenty-four now.

According to the letter from Mark Horn, the lawyer, Paxton and his brother, Gary, must appear together to claim Joshua's quarter of land. Horn would have notified Gary of the inheritance too.

Apparently, Gary Wirth was already here in Monotony looking for Paxton. It didn't appear that Mark Horn, who had moved so suddenly to Omaha, had arrived back in Monotony yet. Paxton had to find Gary, and he needed to talk to the lawyer too.

His eyes fell on the barred window. Those bars reminded him that he had something more urgent to do now than find either Gary or the lawyer. That young fellow, Jeff Rooker, had been right. He shouldn't have come to town.

He thrived on excitement but only when he could do something about it. Here he was helpless, a feeling that bred despera-

28

tion inside him. He felt as frantic as those Indians had looked down at Fort Reno. He had anticipated some excitement there if he'd stayed on as a civilian scout. The Cheyennes cooped up at Fort Reno in Oklahoma Territory were dying like flies from a combination of white man's diseases and a climate that did not agree with them. They had threatened to break away and go back to their home in the north. Paxton had felt that they would try it even if it meant death for all of them.

Across the narrow alley, he heard a steady rumble of voices from the pool hall. The talk was getting louder by the minute. Likely a little firewater was increasing the volume of the discussions. Paxton glanced at the western sky. The sun was near the horizon. The mob might not wait until dark.

The sun was down when the sound across the alley burst out the front door of the pool hall and crescendoed to a howl as the men charged down the alley toward the door of the jail. Standing at the window, Paxton saw the cowboy, Vic Ortis, leading the pack. The white-haired man, Norrid, watched from the corner of the pool hall.

Paxton backed away from the window when they reached the jail. He could still see the mob. Ortis took a key out of his pocket and quickly unlocked the door. The deputy, Buskey, was nowhere in sight.

Men burst into the cell and swarmed over Paxton. He got in two solid licks before they mashed him against the cell wall. He guessed there were at least a dozen men in the cell with him.

Paxton's arms were jerked behind his back and a man with a rope bound them together, jerking the rope uncomfortably tight.

"There's a big cottonwood down by the creek behind the blacksmith shop," one man yelled excitedly. "That's far enough to drag him."

"We'll show these gunmen they can't come in here, murder our citizens and get away with it," Ortis shouted.

Paxton was dragged out into the alley and virtually carried across the street and along the side of the blacksmith shop. If anyone in town objected to what was happening, he did it in the quiet of his own thoughts. Paxton knew his minutes were numbered.

Chapter 3

Paxton was propelled past the blacksmith shop to the creek bank where a lone cottonwood tree stood like an outcast from the grove farther up the creek. Someone rode down from the livery barn, leading a saddled horse, and Paxton was heaved unceremoniously into the saddle.

The light was fading fast but Paxton could still see those around him clearly. He recognized some of the faces he had seen at the store today. Elias Norrid, the banker, had followed as far as the blacksmith shop and stopped there, obviously approving of the proceedings but not wanting to dirty his hands in the actual work.

The cowboy, Vic Ortis, was the leader of the action. He gave the orders and others obeyed. There were other cowboys in the mob. Paxton guessed they were buddies of Ortis, probably the ones his friend, Al Zamora, had gathered. Tug Buskey wasn't there. Paxton hadn't expected him to be. This was no place for the law.

Paxton glared at the men around him. He wouldn't give them the satisfaction of seeing how he felt, his insides tied in knots, his stomach as cold as ice. He had faced death several times because he had lived by his gun, both as army scout and hired gun. He'd always had a fighting chance, and he'd never thought of himself as being afraid to die. But this was different. There wasn't a thing he could do to save himself or even to strike back at his tormentors.

He stared up the slope at Norrid standing at the rear of the blacksmith shop. He could barely make him out now in the dusk. His fury centered on the banker. He was like a Roman Emperor, sitting in his high seat, waiting with dignified poise for the excitement when the Christians were thrown to the lions.

Did Norrid know who he really was? Was that why there were ranch hands in the mob? Was Norrid using the coincidence that Paxton looked like the hired killer who had murdered Roy Greer to get the townspeople to hang him?

"Get that rope over here," Ortis yelled at a man on the fringe of the crowd.

"Can't get the knot tied right," came the reply.

"A lot of help you are!" Ortis growled

and stormed through the crowd to the man with the rope.

Paxton felt the cold lump in the pit of his stomach swelling up into his throat until it threatened to choke him. There was no stir in the direction of town. Maybe the town bosses were in the mob so that even if anyone disagreed with the proceedings, he didn't dare object.

Ortis returned, carrying the rope. "Let's get on with it," he shouted as if he were afraid that the hanging mood of the mob might fade if there was much delay.

He threw the rope over a fairly high limb and mounted the horse that the man had ridden from the barn. From there, he slipped the noose over Paxton's head. Dismounting, he fastened the end of the rope to a low limb on the tree so it wouldn't slip. He was making sure there was no mistake by doing everything himself. He'd probably slap the horse out from under Paxton too.

Anger and frustration churned inside Paxton. He'd seen men die at the end of a rope. It was never a pretty sight. It was even worse when the man cried and begged for his life. Paxton would not do that, no matter what the provocation.

Frustration tore at him. He couldn't

cope with helplessness. There hadn't been a thing he could do about his situation since Tug Buskey had appeared on the scene in front of the store today to arrest him.

"Stand back," Ortis shouted.

He stepped to the rear of Paxton's horse. Paxton braced himself for the jerk.

Instead, there came a roar that was deafening in the tense silence. Paxton felt a vicious tug on the rope around his neck. The horse jumped but didn't bolt out from under him.

For just a second, there was a paralyzed silence following the blast. In that instant, Paxton realized that the roar had been a shotgun blast. But who would be shooting? His first thought was that the man had shot at Paxton and missed him by inches, hitting the rope above his head.

Then a voice from the bank of the creek snapped at the stunned crowd. "Don't anybody move except to unbuckle gun belts."

Nobody made any move at all.

"I said, drop those belts!" the voice snapped, and this time, there was an urgency in it that prompted action.

Hands moved and fingers flew as buckles were unhooked and gun belts dropped to the ground. Paxton twisted his head to look at the creek bank. He couldn't see anyone, and he doubted if anyone else could either. If someone like Ortis could have seen the man, he'd have taken a chance on grabbing his gun. But even Ortis unbuckled his gun belt and let it fall.

"Now then back off slow," the voice said.

As the men backed away into a knot a few feet beyond the tree, the man at the creek directed his words at Paxton.

"Mister, can you finish breaking that rope?"

Paxton jerked his head forward and felt the rope give. There was a tightening of the rope around his neck before it snapped.

"Now get off that horse and come down here. Don't get between me and them."

Paxton swung down and managed to land on his feet. Moving in a circle, he got to the creek. There, he saw Jeff Rooker with a shotgun aimed at the knot of men. He scooted over to Rooker. From here, he could barely see the men by the tree.

Rooker laid down the shotgun and, taking a knife from his belt, slashed the rope holding Paxton's wrists.

"Now then," Rooker said softly, "go back up there and pick up those guns.

That will pull their fangs. Bring that horse too. I don't have one for you."

Paxton stood up and went back to the tree in a circular route, keeping well out of Rooker's line of fire. Stooping low, he picked up all the revolvers and rifles he could see in the growing darkness. Ortis swore viciously as Paxton came near him but he didn't risk making a threatening move. Paxton glanced at the blacksmith shop, but he couldn't see Norrid now. He could imagine the hate that must be seething in the banker. He doubted if Elias Norrid was used to being thwarted like this.

With all the guns he could carry, Paxton went back to the horse and led him to the creek.

"Keep a couple of the best guns," Rooker said softly. "And give me a rifle. I can use one. Then ride up the creek."

"What about you?"

"I'll be along."

Paxton mounted and started his horse up the creek. He glanced back just in time to see a couple of the men break from the pack and start toward town, probably for horses and guns. The shotgun boomed and both men dropped like rocks, although Paxton was sure the buckshot had gone over their heads. None of the others moved.

Then Paxton saw some movement along the creek bank behind him. Rooker must be running for his horse now. Paxton kept the horse at a steady lope, holding him down until Rooker could catch up.

Rooker overtook Paxton within a mile of town. He spurred past Paxton, motioning for him to come on. Paxton nudged his horse into a gallop. In a short time, he was riding beside Rooker.

"Think they'll follow us?" he asked.

"Sure as a turpentined dog will run," Rooker said. "They won't crowd us too close, though. They have a healthy respect for this scatter gun."

"Maybe you should have kept them peaceable with a few more blasts," Paxton suggested.

"Couldn't," Rooker said easily. "I had only two shells. I used both of them."

"Why did you open the game with only two shells?"

"A shotgun speaks with a loud voice," Rooker said. "I had to get their attention."

"But it's no good to you now if they catch us."

"I wouldn't say that. A lot of big pots have been won on a pair of deuces when the other fellow thought they were aces." He held up the shotgun. "Looks loaded, doesn't it?"

Paxton grinned. "I wouldn't argue with it if I didn't know it was empty."

Rooker kept twisting in the saddle to look back. It was too dark to see anything. Paxton strained his ears but could hear nothing over the thunder of their own horses' hoofs.

Rooker reined down and Paxton stopped. With everything still, they listened. The unmistakable pound of horses came from down the creek.

"You ride on," Rooker said. "There's an old abandoned homestead ahead about a mile. Put your horse in the barn there and hide. They may not find you. I may be able to bluff them into going back."

"You've risked enough for me already," Paxton said.

"I'm enjoying it," Rooker said. "Don't spoil my fun now by being a brave fool."

Paxton nodded. Rooker really did seem to be enjoying his act. Nudging his horse into a gallop, he headed on up the creek. He hoped nothing would happen to Rooker. If Paxton had a friend in this country, it had to be this young fellow with the sparkling, black eyes. At least Rooker was well armed, having selected a good rifle from the stack Paxton had brought down to the creek from the tree. Paxton had taken a revolver and holster.

Finding the abandoned homestead, Paxton put his horse in the barn, only a short distance from the house. The doors on the barn were gone and he didn't take time to tie the horse. He might have to leave in a hurry.

He ran to the house, noting that the doors and windows were gone there too. The house was a mansion compared to the dugouts on most homesteads. It was built of cottonwood logs, and some of the logs touching the ground had begun to rot. It didn't take cottonwood long to rot when exposed to moisture and dirt.

Stepping inside, he tried to penetrate the darkness. A red blotch against one wall caught his attention and, stepping closer, he discovered a calf that had gotten inside and died. It looked like it had been about a three hundred pound animal, already disintegrating. The odor was enough to make him consider going on, but then he heard the thunder of hoofbeats. Riders charged into the yard and yanked to a halt in front of the house.

"Al, look in the barn," a man yelled. "Vic, check the house."

Paxton was cornered. Apparently, Rooker hadn't been able to slow the mob. No telling what had happened to him. There was little doubt what would happen to Paxton if they got their hands on him again. He had little chance of holding them off.

Watching the two men dismount to search the barn and house, he pulled the gun out of the holster and thumbed back the hammer. The gun felt good in his hand, but it wasn't his own and he sensed the difference. The men out there couldn't have taken time to collect many guns or they wouldn't have been this close behind him.

The darkness hid the features of the men but not their movements. Paxton could only aim in the general direction of the man coming toward the house and squeeze the trigger. The man wheeled almost in mid-stride and dashed back to the horses. The man approaching the barn ducked low and retreated at full speed.

From somewhere among the riders, two guns blasted away at the house. Paxton ducked low, thinking that maybe he had a chance against only two guns. He fired twice more at the men clustered in the yard and they scattered like quail.

The return shots came from two different spots now and Paxton answered them, reloading when his gun was empty. Then he heard noises at both ends of the cottonwood log cabin. There wasn't a window at either end but he could guess what was going on. While he'd been exchanging shots with the two gunmen, other men had circled around and come up to the cabin on the windowless ends and were now busy starting fires to burn him out.

The acrid smell of smoke verified his guess. This was one kind of fight he couldn't win. Cottonwood burned like dry paper and this house would soon be a blazing inferno. If he stayed here, he would be roasted alive. If he dashed out, he'd be picked off by the two gunmen who would have him silhouetted against the burning building. He had no more chance of escaping this inferno than he would if he'd been a snowball.

Chapter 4

As the flames exploded up the ends of the cabin, Paxton backed off from the front window. The fire was lighting up the yard some now. Soon it would break through into the interior of the cabin. Then if he were near a window, he would be silhouetted like a bird on a tree limb.

He crossed to the back of the room but found a blank wall there. Then he remembered. As he had ridden up, he had noted that the house and barn were both built right against the bluff flanking the creek. The chalk bluff formed the back wall of the barn and the cabin's rear wall was laid up right against the bluff. There would be no escaping out the back of the house.

So that left only the front, and there were a dozen men and at least two guns waiting for him there. He felt like a fox trapped in the corner of a barn.

The longer he waited to make a break, the less chance he'd have of succeeding. There had been no shots fired since the fire blazed up. They were content to wait. Either Paxton came out or he died in the fire.

The dry wood snapped at one end of the cabin, and a log was jarred out of place. Flame licked through the opening and up the inside of the wall. The interior of the cabin was bathed in flickering light. Paxton stayed well back from the door and windows. They wouldn't get any shots at him until he made his break.

While moving away from the fire at one end of the cabin, his foot hit a board in the floor that sagged and squealed from his weight. He looked down at his feet. The board next to the one he had stepped on was splintered where some heavy animal had broken through. His eyes flipped to the decaying carcass of the calf along the back wall. Maybe that calf had broken a leg when it fell through the floor and couldn't get out of the house.

Then the absurdity of it struck him. How could a calf break through a floor that was laid directly on the ground? He bent over and examined the floor where he had stepped and where the calf had broken through. Rapping on the boards, he heard a hollow echo.

Dropping on his knees, he quickly examined the floor, and partly by feel and partly by the light from the fire, he found the edge of a trap door. Running his hand quickly along the seam, he found an iron ring under two inches of dirt and debris. He pushed the dirt away then grasped the ring and pulled. The door lifted, revealing a hole almost three feet square beneath the floor. It appeared to be at least four feet deep.

Swinging his feet over the hole, he lowered himself into it. He had no time to wonder what the hole was doing there or what might be in it. The fire was licking up both ends of the house now and the heat was becoming intense.

When his feet hit the bottom, he found that his head stuck up only about a foot above the floor. Squatting, he discovered a tunnel running off in the direction of the barn.

He knew then what this was. He'd been in a couple of the old Butterfield Overland Despatch stations along the Smoky Hill River in Kansas. Several of those stations had tunnels connecting the station and the barn, and several had tunnels running out from the station to little forts about five feet square. These had roofs over the tops which were held up by chunks of sod or wood and were only about six or eight inches above the level of the prairie. A man standing in one of those holes at the end of a tunnel could hold off a horde of Indians while remaining comparatively safe from Indian bullets and arrows. The Indians had quickly learned to respect and avoid those little forts at the end of the tunnels. Apparently, whoever had homesteaded this place had dug a tunnel to his barn for defense purposes. There might be tunnels branching out in other directions too, but Paxton wasn't interested in that now.

He dropped on his hands and knees and felt around the tunnel. It seemed to be clear. Paxton had feared it was caved in. He hoped it would be clear far enough so that he could get out from under the burning house.

Reaching back, he pulled the door down over the hole to keep out the heat and smoke as long as possible. It was pitch dark inside the tunnel, but there was only one way that Paxton could go.

He made slow progress, feeling his way forward, not having any idea what lay ahead. Whatever it was, it couldn't be any worse than what lay behind him.

As he passed under the wall of the cabin, he felt the warmth seeping down from the fire above. Then it cooled as he moved on. He was outside the walls of the cabin. Here he stopped. He'd have to stay in the tunnel until the fire burned out and the ashes cooled unless he could find an opening at the other end of this tunnel. It might be that it came out at the barn or it might be that the homesteader had just dug the tunnel for refuge in case of Indian attack and the tunnel had only the one opening.

The fire above became a low roar that he could hear. Heat and a little smoke filtered into the tunnel. The floor above the tunnel must be burning now. He found it hard not to cough even though there was only a little smoke. He felt a light draft and the smoke got no worse. It must be drifting past him. That would mean that it was finding an exit somewhere ahead.

He stretched out on the tunnel floor and the smoke drifted by above his head. He was glad that the wood was dry cotton-wood which gave off very little smoke. Cottonwood burned with great intensity but didn't last long.

When the fire burned down and the heat no longer filtered into the tunnel, he found it chilly on the damp ground. He crawled slowly back toward the house. The ground was warm under the cabin. He could hear sounds somewhere above, apparently out in the yard.

He wondered if the fire had burned the trap door away and allowed the opening of the tunnel to show, but there was no light coming into the tunnel. The chances were that the roof and debris had fallen over the hole and covered it even if the fire had burned all the floor.

He still heard men's voices out in the yard, but the ashes would be too hot to examine for a while so he had no fear of being discovered now. He stretched out on the ground that had been heated by the fire and dropped off to sleep.

A thumping sound directly above woke him. He had no idea how long he had been asleep. It could very well be morning. Men's voices drifted down to him, but only when they spoke loudly could he understand what they said. He lay still, fearful that any movement he made would be heard above. He did inch his hand down and get his gun out of the holster. If they discovered the tunnel, they'd have to come down to get him, and he'd get one of them at least before they got him.

The thumping continued above as men scrambled over the debris left by the fire. Apparently, the fire hadn't burned all the floor because he distinctly heard boots hit wood now and then. Then suddenly a man yelled.

"Hey, I've found him. Here's his bones. Burned pretty bad."

"That was a hot fire," another man said, moving toward the first speaker.

Paxton realized that they must have found the charred skeleton of the big calf. Maybe they couldn't tell it was an animal's bones. They were looking for the burned skeleton of a man, and apparently, they were satisfied that they had found it.

"Well, that's the end of that gunman," one man declared with satisfaction.

Paxton lay still and listened for more sounds. There was some scrambling as the men left the ashes, and then it was quiet. Paxton stirred, moving down the tunnel away from the house. The opening into the house was obviously covered or the searchers would have found it.

He crawled until he hit a wall. A touch of panic seized him. Was this the end of the tunnel? He shoved on the wall and discovered that it was not dirt. It felt like hay, and it moved when he pushed it.

In a moment, he had pushed the hay away from the end of the tunnel and found himself looking into the barn where he had put his horse the night before. The horse was gone; apparently, the raiders had taken him. It had been their horse, anyway. He crawled out into the stable and stretched his muscles. He had lain cramped in that tunnel a long time. The sun was shining brightly just outside the barn, but he waited until his eyes were accustomed to the brightness before stepping to the opening that had been a door.

He stopped there. A couple of riders were still in sight of the burned house. Turning back, he looked over the interior of the barn. The barn was built of sod. No one would burn it. The hay could easily be pushed back against the tunnel opening or even tied into a bale and pulled into place after a man crawled inside. This would make a good hideout for him until he could learn who had murdered Joshua and Roy Greer and settle the score with them. Then he must locate his brother so they could claim their inheritance.

He had lost all his supplies when Buskey had arrested him yesterday. He was hungry, but where could he find anything to eat out here?

After making sure that everyone had left the scene of the fire, he went outside and walked quickly to the creek, then turned upstream. He didn't want to go back to town, at least, not yet. First, he needed to find out who was behind the scheme to kill him and why. If he wasn't careful, he could be dead before he learned the truth.

The creek was only a small trickle here. Roy had written that Cottonwood Creek was just a little stream that ran into a bigger one beyond Monotony. There were chalk bluffs along the creek. In some places, they reached as high as thirty feet above the creek. Holes were in the bluffs, some big enough to be called caves. The possibility of hiding in one of those caves if things got desperate entered Paxton's mind.

The spring where Joshua Greer had homesteaded must be somewhere near here, Paxton reasoned, remembering the few things that Roy had written. But what Paxton needed now was food. He hadn't eaten anything since the snack he'd had yesterday just before he got to Monotony.

He walked about a mile when he saw a little dugout burrowed into the bluff on the bench above the creek bottom. He studied it for a while. It looked as though it might be lived in. It had a good front door and a tiny window beside it. But most of the house, if there was much to it, had been dug back into the bluff.

After watching the dugout for ten minutes and seeing no sign of life, Paxton moved cautiously away from the creek and up to the door. He knocked, but there was no sound inside.

He knocked again then tried the door. It pushed open at his touch and light streamed into the one room. A table, a couple of chairs and a bed seemed to be all the furniture. A stove sat near the front of the room where the stovepipe could angle out above the door. Paxton stepped inside, leaving the door open so light would come in. He doubted if the little window would let much light inside if the door was shut. He saw the shelves along one wall and moved to them.

The shelves were back out of the direct light from the door, and he couldn't see very well. He could make out enough to know that the shelves were almost empty, but there was enough there to take the edge off his appetite.

He had just picked up some bread when the doorway darkened. He wheeled, the bread in his gun hand. He had no chance to defend himself.

Chapter 5

"Hold it or you're dead!" the man in the doorway shouted.

Paxton didn't move. The voice was familiar. He knew that the man couldn't see much, just coming in out of the brilliant sunlight outside, but he would be able to see if Paxton moved.

When the man stepped out of the doorway to let in more light, Paxton heaved a sigh of relief.

"Jeff! I'm glad to see it's you."

Jeff Rooker slowly lowered his gun. "I figured you for dead after I saw what they did to that cabin. How did you give them the slip?"

"Did you know about the tunnel between the house and the barn?"

Rooker shook his head. "Never heard of it. I doubt if anybody else ever did, either. An old bachelor named Brandt took that homestead. Couldn't make a go of it and left. He must have been afraid of Indians."

"I'm glad he was part prairie dog.

Without that tunnel, I'd have been roasted."

Rooker shut the door and lit a candle on the table. It gave enough light that they could see around the room. "I thought I was seeing a ghost when I recognized you," he admitted. "I met a man from town a mile or so back. He said they told him that they'd found your bones burned in the cabin."

"That was a calf that died in the cabin," Paxton explained.

"You must have spent a pleasant night in that tunnel."

"Better than out of it, I'll guarantee," Paxton said. "How come they didn't shoot you on sight after what you did?"

"Because they don't know who used that scatter gun on them," Rooker said with a grin. "They do know I sure wouldn't lift a finger to keep Roy Greer's killer from stretching a rope so they won't suspect me."

"Some of them surely must know that I'm not the man who killed Roy," Paxton said.

"Maybe. But even those men wouldn't suspect me of helping a total stranger."

Paxton nodded. "Come to think of it, I'm not sure myself why you did."

"You said you were a close friend of Roy's. That puts us on the same side."

53

Rooker's face darkened. "The Circle N was in that mob set on hanging you. I figure the Circle N had Pa killed. I've got that score to settle if I can find the killer or the man who hired him."

"You saw the man who killed Roy. Did he really look like me?"

"Like two peas in a pod. At least, at first glance. I can see quite a difference when I study you a while."

"What happened to you last night after I left you?"

"I made a lot of noise to get them to chase me. But they caught on that I wasn't the one they were after and only a couple of them chased me while the rest went on after you. I gave the two chasing me the slip. I don't think they liked the idea of chasing me anyway. They wanted in on the fun of running you down."

"I guess I spoiled their fun."

"They don't think so. They think you burned in that fire." Jeff Rooker's black eyes sparkled. "I've got an idea. I thought I was looking at a ghost when I saw you. I reckon those who burned that house would think the same."

Paxton frowned. "A ghost?"

Rooker laughed. "Sure. Maybe it's crazy, but then Pa always said I'd never make a farmer because I wouldn't take anything serious. If I can't find something to laugh at, I'd just as soon be dead."

Paxton studied Jeff Rooker. He was half a foot shorter than Paxton and weighed less than a hundred and fifty pounds; he had black eyes and almost black hair, with mischief and the love of life lighting his small features. He didn't look as if he had a serious bone in his body.

"Right now I'm a hungry ghost," Paxton said.

"We can take care of that. I brought in a couple of prairie chickens. I was hunting when I met that fellow from town." He went to the stove and started a fire. "How does being a ghost strike you?"

"Have to think about it," Paxton said.

"It might help keep you alive. You've attracted the attention of a lot of people who are itching to kill you."

"Nobody's going to believe in a ghost walking around or riding a horse," Paxton said.

"I ain't so sure," Rooker said as he picked up the prairie chickens he had dropped just inside the door.

"Let's dress these chickens. Some people scald them and pick the feathers off. I just skin them."

Outside, he handed one bird to Paxton while he tackled the other with his knife. "Bertha Norrid has a lot of people believing in spirits," he said. "Ghosts ain't much different, I reckon."

"Spirits? You mean, she's a medium?" Paxton slit the skin along the leg of his bird.

"That's what she calls herself," Rooker said. "Never heard of such a thing myself. She claims the spirits tell her what is going to happen, and she's been right so often that people are about ready to believe anything she says."

"Norrid? Any relation to that white-headed banker?"

"She's his sister," Rooker said. "Elias Norrid owns a big share of this country. Ran the Circle N till he decided he could gouge more people if he was running a bank, so he started one in Monotony. Bertha is an old maid and has kept house for her brother since his wife died. She cooks up more seances than she does grub."

"Does she really believe in that?"

"You bet she does. She claims she can call the spirits back to talk to people on earth. Old Elias don't go for it, but a lot of people do. Her closest follower is the

56

preacher, Oscar Sutcliffe. Working together, they have converted a lot of people. Everybody's pretty well spooked. It won't be hard to convince them that a ghost is running loose in the valley. That ghost could haunt a bunch of people who thought they saw him burn."

Paxton saw his point, but he wasn't ready to believe that the idea was practical. "They might be jumpy enough to shoot at the ghost."

"Maybe," Rooker admitted. "But if they think you're not a ghost, they'll start shooting sure as sunrise."

The more Rooker talked, the less crazy the idea sounded. Pretending to be a live ghost was surely better than being a dead gunman.

"Where is this spring where Joshua Greer had his homestead?" he asked.

"Up the creek about a mile," Rooker said. "It's not a homestead: it's a pre-emption. He paid it off in a year. After Pa was killed, I worked for Joshua. Roy came just a week before Joshua was killed. Roy stayed, and so did I. When Roy was killed, I moved into this abandoned dugout."

When the prairie chickens were cleaned and washed with water from the creek, Jeff Rooker led the way back into the dugout.

The stove was hot, so he put in more fuel, put grease in his skillet and cut up one of the birds to fry.

"The Circle N uses this land, but they don't own it so they can't throw me out," Rooker said. "That spring of Joshua's is the start of the water flow for Cottonwood Creek. The Circle N used it for watering their cattle till Joshua took out papers on it and fenced off the spring. Norrid and Tidrow were mad as hornets about that, and I figure they had him killed. When Roy refused to leave, they hired this gunman to kill him. If I'd stayed, I'd have got it too."

"I suppose the Circle N claims the spring now."

"They never stopped claiming it. They called Joshua and Roy squatters. They tore down that fence first thing."

"You think Norrid hired the killer?"

Rooker looked sharply at Paxton. "I shouldn't be running off at the mouth like this, but I figure either Norrid or Tidrow did. Sam Tidrow was Norrid's foreman; then when Norrid moved to town, Tidrow became his manager. It's Tidrow's daughter, Loanda, who lives in Joshua's house now."

"Tidrow's daughter? Does she have a family?"

"She ain't even married. She's old enough and pretty enough to get a man, but she's either too stubborn or too stuck-up for any cowboy to dab a loop on her. She's holding that spring for the Circle N, though, and it'll take a good man to get it away from her."

When the prairie chicken was done, Rooker forked it out onto two plates, and they sat down at the crude table to eat.

"Do you know who killed Joshua?" Paxton asked as he began on the chicken.

Rooker shook his head, his mouth full. "No idea," he said when he could talk. "He was shot in the back down by the spring. I got a good look at the man who shot Roy, though. I was sure I was seeing him again when I saw you. Reckon others thought so too."

"Would you know this killer if you saw him again?"

"I'd know him sure as sunrise. You figure on going after him?"

"I came here to help Roy and to meet my brother. According to our lawyer, Gary and I are to inherit Joshua's place but we have to appear together to get it. One thing seems clear. If we're going to survive on Joshua's land, we'll have to eliminate the man who killed Roy and probably Joshua too."

"If this man they call Kucek is the one

who killed Roy, you'd better be fast if you plan to face him," Rooker said. "He's a slick hand with a gun. He got into a fight in Monotony, and people are still talking about how fast he was."

"I've worked six years as either an army scout or a hired gun," Paxton said quietly. "I've seen some bad ones, and I'm still here to talk about it."

Rooker's eyes widened. "No wonder Roy sent for you."

"Roy knew what I did for a living," Paxton said. "I'm just sorry I didn't get here in time. Have you heard of a man named Gary Wirth?"

Rooker nodded. "I've heard the name in town. Are you looking for him?"

"He's my real brother. We were orphaned when I was four and Gary was two. The Greers raised me and they seem like my real family. Gary was adopted by a family named Wirth. I haven't seen him since. He is supposed to meet me here at Monotony."

"I'll ride into town and ask," Rooker volunteered. "I ain't got nothing better to do. You keep your pretty face out of sight. We'll pick the time and place to show you off as a ghost."

"I didn't come up here to hide," Paxton said. "I'm going up and take a look at

Joshua's spring. A walk will do me good."

"Won't do your health any good if somebody sees you," Rooker objected. "That spring is claimed by the Circle N now."

"I'm just going to look, not take squatter's rights," Paxton said.

"Pa had an old saddle horse that I turned loose," Rooker said as he went outside. "If I can find him, I'll bring him back so you'll have something to ride."

Rooker rode down the valley, and Paxton headed up the creek. If he followed it, he had to come to the spring. Rooker had said it was the source of this creek. If there was no water beyond that, it was no wonder that the Circle N wanted the spring. That was no excuse for murder, though.

Paxton wondered who had killed Joshua. If the gunman, Kucek, had been hired to kill Roy, it seemed likely that he had probably been hired to kill Joshua too. It was possible that Elias Norrid had ordered his ranch manager, Tidrow, to do it. Or maybe Norrid had done it himself. He looked like the kind who expected to get everything he wanted, and he'd probably fight, even kill, to get it.

The stream running steadily beside him was little more than a trickle. It was bigger down by Monotony. There were probably springs seeping into it all along the way.

He kept an eye roving ahead and to either side. He was a marked man in this country. A lot of people seemed to want him dead. He didn't know whether they thought he was the gunman, Kucek, or knew who he really was.

Suddenly he caught a flash near the bluff to his right, and he dropped to the ground. Instant reactions to warnings like that had kept him alive for the past six years. But there was no place out in this open meadow to hide.

He began rolling frantically toward the creek, several yards away. The first bullet missed, snapping the air above him. But the second one hit him low in the shoulder like the blow of an ax. He stopped rolling, the power to move seeming suddenly to vanish. The thought washed over him that it didn't make any difference, anyway. He wasn't going to walk away from this.

He was vaguely aware of a man with a rifle coming down from the bluffs. He lay as still as possible, barely breathing. The man stopped halfway between the bluff and the spot where Paxton lay. He looked apprehensively both ways, then turned and hurried back.

Paxton tried to move enough to get a good look at the man but the world began spinning and then turned black.

Chapter 6

Paxton first realized that he was still alive when someone kneeling beside him touched his face. With an extreme effort, he opened his eyes. The face above him was blurred and so out of focus that he first thought it was the face of a woman.

He closed his eyes then pried them open again. He saw the same face only it was clearer this time. It was the face of a young woman, and she was studying him intently.

"Glad you're still kicking," she said softly. "I thought maybe I was working on a lost cause. I made a travois to pull you behind my horse. You'll have to help me get you on it."

He found it almost impossible to move and when he did, a searing pain shot through his shoulder and chest. That pain drove the fog from his brain, and he gasped for breath.

"Can you move your legs?" the girl asked.

Paxton worked his legs to prove that they

still operated. His vision was clearing, but the pain didn't subside. Even though the girl was small, when she got her hands under his arms, she was able to drag him toward the travois. He pumped his legs to help her but the pain almost made him pass out again.

Then he was on the travois and the horse began moving. Paxton thought the stabbing pain associated with every step the horse took would tear him apart. The travois seemed to find every bump in the meadow.

The horse finally stopped. Again, Paxton responded to the girl's demand that he help himself. He saw now how small she really was, almost a foot shorter than he was. She was strong, however, and determined.

She kicked backward to push open the door into the house and dragged him inside. The cot where she put him was low, and she managed to get him on it with some help from Paxton, himself. As he sank down on the cot, the world turned black again.

Pain shot through him, and he fought to regain consciousness only to sink deeper into the black pit. He roused after a particularly sharp burst of pain to hear the girl say she thought he'd pull through. He doubted it, but he didn't have the strength to tell her so.

After what seemed like hours of drifting in and out of the peaceful oblivion, awareness of the pain and his surroundings returned. The girl was fussing over him.

"Able to eat something this morning?" she asked.

He tried to shake his head. "I ought to be dead."

"I agree," she said cheerfully. "But you're not, thanks to me. I dug the bullet out and poured in some whiskey. I think you'll make it. Who shot you?"

"Didn't see him," Paxton said weakly. "Don't you know?"

"I can't even guess who shot you or why," she said. "He came mighty close to doing you in. But you looked worth saving to me."

"Who are you?" he asked. "Where did you bring me?"

"I'm Loanda Tidrow, and I brought you to my place. Where else? Especially since you were miles from any ranch."

His mind was clearing rapidly. So he was at Joshua's spring and this was the daughter of the manager of the Circle N ranch. It was an ironic twist.

She brought a pan of soup from the stove and started feeding him. "You might tell me who you are."

"Dave Paxton," he said, wincing at the scalding hot soup.

He watched her face, but if she recognized the name, she didn't let it show.

"I should thank you for what you've done," he said when he finished the soup. "The way I hurt, though, I'm not sure I am thankful."

"As long as you hurt, you're not dead," she said cheerfully. "I've got some riding to do. You'll be all right here."

Her statement left no room for argument. He was left to himself. She bobbed into the house three times during the day to check on him and to feed him more soup. He was too weak to object to anything she did.

In a couple of days, he found that he could move around some although his left arm and shoulder were useless. Within a few days, he was sitting on the edge of the bed and able to do some things for himself. Loanda had his arm in a sling.

Loanda was gone every day, but she was there during the evenings. He found himself looking forward to those evenings. The long quiet days were monotonous. He found it hard to equate Loanda with the proud, stubborn girl Rooker had described. He wondered if it had been someone from the Circle N who had shot him. That would make it even stranger that Loanda Tidrow would be the one who had saved him. If she let them know that he was here, they might show up any time to finish the job.

He was walking slowly around the cabin one evening when she returned. She watched him for a minute.

"You're soon going to be ready to leave the nest," she said with admiration.

"I've been bothering you long enough," he replied. "Have you told your pa that I'm here?"

"Are you crazy?" she demanded. "Pa would shoot me and you both if he knew I was keeping a man in my house, even if he is an invalid. Besides, I don't think they'd welcome me helping you under any circumstances."

He stared at her. She must have learned who Dave Paxton was. "Then why are you doing it?"

"Maybe it's because I do what I want to do. Like I said, you looked like you were worth saving so I gave it a whirl."

"What if I am someone your pa wants dead?"

She shrugged. "Then he's going to have to do the killing; I'm not. Looks to me like it will be a few days yet before you're ready to go out on your own."

Paxton knew she was right, but he intended to get out as quickly as possible, not only for his own safety but for Loanda's sake as well. If her father found him here, she could be in almost as much trouble as he would be. She might be a stubborn, arrogant girl as Rooker said, but she had saved his life. Now he owed her every possible consideration.

Paxton didn't know where Loanda went during the day. It might be home to the Circle N. He was sure that her only responsibility here was to make certain no one else settled on this spring and claimed it like Roy Greer had done after Joshua was killed.

Paxton took advantage of her absence to do some investigating when he got so he could move around the house. There were some unanswered questions in his mind. Why had Roy Greer stayed on after Joshua was killed? He and Roy had played together as boys even though Roy was five years older. He thought he knew Roy pretty well. He had never seen any streak of bravery in him. He must have had a powerful attraction to the land to hold him here.

In his letter, Roy hadn't said why he was staying, only that he was afraid he'd be killed if he did stay. With Joshua, it was different. He was a fighter, a bullheaded man who would never let anyone push him around, even if it meant he might die because of his stubbornness. Paxton could understand how it happened that Joshua had been killed, but not Roy.

The house had two rooms. The room where Paxton had his cot was the living room. It had a barrel stove where Joshua must have burned the cottonwood logs and sticks that were left from the grove the spring after he had built this house. The other room was the kitchen. It was heated by a small cook stove. Loanda had stretched a rope across the living room and dropped a sheet over it to give both Paxton and herself some privacy.

Paxton hadn't been in the kitchen yet but today, moving unsteadily on weakened legs, he crossed to the partition doorway. Loanda's mark was on the kitchen; Joshua wouldn't have left it this neat. As Paxton remembered him when he made his home with John and Elisa Greer, Paxton's foster parents, he wasn't particularly neat.

There had always been a mystery about Joshua Greer. He only stayed at the home of his brother, John, in eastern Kansas about half the time. The rest of the time he was off on some escapade which he never explained when he returned. On his return once, however, he admitted that he'd gotten married while he was gone. But the widow he'd married had an almost grown son, and the two of them had run him crazy until he'd pulled his freight one night. Where he'd been the other times was a secret he kept to himself.

Josh had always kept a "possibles" bag with him which he never let anyone look into. The worst whipping Paxton had gotten as a boy had been for starting to open that bag. Later Josh had given Paxton a bag of candy, something almost unheard of on the Greer farm, and Paxton had forgotten about the whipping and remembered the candy. He didn't forget to stay away from Uncle Josh's "possibles" bag, though. He wondered if Josh's secrets had died with him or if he had hidden them somewhere. Maybe Roy had learned some of those secrets.

Suddenly he thought of Roy's letter. His hand dived to the pocket where he'd had it. It was still there. He found it hard to believe that Loanda had not found that. If she had, then she knew who he was and why he was here. If she knew he was here to take possession of this land by the spring, why hadn't she killed him or told her father? He'd have done it, if Rooker's assessment of Sam Tidrow was accurate. Maybe she hadn't found it. If she hadn't, it showed more restraint on Loanda's part than he'd have given her credit for. She'd had the perfect chance to go through his pockets while he was helpless.

He remembered the last line in Roy's letter, and he took the letter out and read it again to be sure he was recalling it right. "If I'm not here when you come, the stump will be our mailbox," he read.

Putting the letter back in his pocket, he went to the outside door. There were a dozen stumps not far from the house, all that remained of the cottonwood grove that had once stood by the spring.

He wondered if he had strength enough now to walk out to those stumps after spending so much time flat on his back in bed. Curiosity and a sense of urgency drove him to try. One of those stumps should have a message for him if Roy had had a chance to put it there.

Leaving the house, he moved toward the

stumps. He recalled the game he and Roy had played at home, leaving notes for each other in some secret place they called their mailbox. Roy hadn't forgotten.

Several of the stumps showed new ax marks. Joshua and Roy must have been grubbing some of them out for firewood for the coming winter. There was one stump bigger around and cut a little higher than the others. Paxton made for it. Roy hadn't designated which stump; he had just called it "the stump." That big one must surely be "the stump."

The big stump had no new ax marks on it. It had heavy roots running out from its base. It had supported a huge tree. Remembering how Roy used to hide his notes, Paxton dropped on his knees and began feeling under those heavy roots. The second one he probed beneath yielded a little roll of papers.

Spreading the papers out, he discovered there were several clippings from newspapers. His eyes widened as he looked. Joshua's secret life was there before him. He no longer wondered why Josh guarded his "possibles" bag so closely if he carried things like this in it.

The biggest clipping was from the front page of an Omaha newspaper. It told of a train robbery near Big Springs on the

Union Pacific two and a half years ago. There had been six robbers, according to reports, but only three had been caught and none of the money recovered. The captured bandits had said that the money had been buried at night near a spring.

Racing his eyes over the other clippings, Paxton saw that they were all about the robbery. Things began dropping into place. These clippings hadn't been in Josh's bag when he'd given Paxton the whipping, but there had probably been others similar to this. Paxton knew now where Josh had been on those trips that kept him away for weeks. Josh had been one of the three train robbers who hadn't been caught. This spring was the one where Joshua thought they had buried the money. He had come here and filed on the land with the spring.

The holes around the spring had probably been dug by people other than Joshua who had read this item in the paper and guessed that this was the spring. If Joshua had left shortly after coming here, he'd have been suspected of being one of the robbers and trailed. But by filing on the land and staying here, he would not arouse suspicions. Josh had always been the careful one. He also loved this land he had preempted, Paxton knew from letters he had received from his foster parents.

Two questions still plagued Paxton. Had Joshua found the money? It seemed reasonable that he would have if it was still here when he came. And who had killed him? He'd been sure it had been someone from the Circle N — or at least someone hired by the Circle N. But now he wondered. Could it have been one of the other members of the gang? There had been six and only three had been caught, the report said. Who were the other two, and had they been involved in Joshua's murder?

He guessed now why Roy Greer had stayed on. Roy had learned Josh's secret. He had stayed, trying to find that money, and it cost him his life. Was Kucek, the man who killed Roy, a member of the gang or just someone the Circle N had hired? He had more questions now than he'd had before he found the papers.

He stuffed the clippings back into the space under the tree root.

Trouble came a couple of days later. Paxton sensed its approach by the uneasiness in Loanda. She didn't ride out that day as usual. Paxton and Loanda hadn't agreed on everything but their truce, if it could be called that, had grown into a kind of bond that Paxton didn't want to break.

This morning Loanda watched the window and Paxton did too. He saw Elias Norrid as soon as she did. Loanda went out and met the white-haired banker in the yard. They argued sharply, but she refused to let him come in. Paxton waited expectantly, his hand on his gun.

Norrid left and he was barely out of sight when Tidrow and his two gun hands, Al Zamora and Vic Ortis, rode over the hill from the southeast. Something obviously had alerted Tidrow and Norrid that someone might be with Loanda at the spring.

Loanda turned her father and the two gunmen away too, but Vic Ortis watched the house like a hunting hawk until he left. He didn't believe whatever Loanda was telling them.

Shortly after they left, Loanda herself rode away. Paxton immediately began packing his things. He was able to take care of himself now, and he had to get out of here and leave no trace that he'd ever been here.

He was almost to the door when he glanced out the window and saw a rider pulling in behind the barn. He recognized Vic Ortis. He was coming back to check things out for himself.

Ortis might watch from the barn to see if there was any movement around the house, or he might come on in to investigate. Paxton wasn't sure how a fight with Ortis would go. Ortis was a gunman, and he'd be primed for a battle if he came to the house.

Judging from the way Ortis had performed at the jail and at the aborted hanging, he was not a patient man. He'd be coming to the house soon. Paxton braced himself for a showdown.

Chapter 7

Paxton looked around for some means of giving himself a slight edge when Ortis came in. Fairness was not the name of the game when Ortis was involved. To get into the house, he'd surely come in the front door.

Paxton's eyes stopped on the shelf above the door where Loanda had put a clock. He doubted if Joshua had built that shelf there for a clock. Paxton saw a way that might distract Ortis for a moment when he charged in. A moment might be long enough to give Paxton the advantage, perhaps a big enough advantage that there wouldn't be any gun battle at all. Ortis was gunman enough to know when not to push his luck.

Quickly, Paxton lifted the clock off the shelf and grabbed the pail that Loanda kept water in. Emptying some of the water in a basin, he tied a small rope he found in the corner to the bail of the bucket.

He glanced out the window and saw Ortis peeking around the corner of the

barn, apparently watching for any movement. If he didn't see any, he'd come to investigate before long.

Setting the bucket on the shelf, he tied
the other end of the rope to the door knob.
He wished he could test it to see how far
the door would have to open before the
bucket came off the shelf. But there was no
chance for a test. He had to guess. That
bucket crashing down on Ortis's head
ought to shatter his concentration.

He finished his task and stepped back
against the far wall. He was just in time to
see Ortis dashing silently across the yard
from the barn. Paxton braced himself but
Ortis didn't charge in. He was going to see
what was inside first.

Paxton slipped behind the sheet Loanda
had put up in front of his cot. From one
corner of the sheet, he watched the door
and windows. He saw Ortis look in one
window then move to the door.

The second he heard the door hinge
move, Paxton stepped out. Ortis banged
the door open and charged in. The pail
was jerked off the shelf and tipped over by
the pull of the rope tied to the door knob.
The water and the bucket hit Ortis at exactly the same instant. Ortis had his gun in
his hand, eyes sweeping the room, when

the bucket crashed down over his head.

Ortis squalled like a rabbit caught in a snare. His bellow reverberated in the bucket which fit down over his head to his shoulders.

Paxton crossed the room in three long leaps, grabbed the gun out of Ortis's hand and slammed his own gun against the side of the bucket. Ortis screamed, which only added to the terrific din inside the bucket. Ortis tried to get his hands up to jerk the bucket off his head but Paxton grabbed them and beat a steady tattoo on the bucket. Ortis sank to the floor, apparently rendered almost senseless by the noise. Paxton could only imagine what the din must be inside that bucket.

Jerking the end of the rope off the door-knob, Paxton pulled Ortis's hands behind his back and lashed them together. Then, he pulled the bucket down tightly enough so that it couldn't be rubbed off his head. Ortis sat on the floor almost in a stupor.

Paxton gathered the things he was going to take with him and went to the door. Before he left he gave the bucket a few more hard bangs with the barrel of his gun. Loanda wasn't going to appreciate the dents in her bucket, but she'd appreciate that more than having Paxton discovered in her house. When Loanda found Ortis, she'd get him out from under the bucket. Even if Ortis didn't believe that he had surprised a robber in the house, he certainly wouldn't be able to prove that it wasn't so.

Once outside the house, Paxton moved down the creek toward Rooker's place. He was still weak, but he had exercised enough the last few days so that he was coming back to normal. His shoulder was still sore, but Loanda had doctored the wound well. He owed her his life.

Rooker saw Paxton and came out to meet him. "Thought you were dead," he said in disbelief, "even if I couldn't find the remains."

"Would be if Loanda Tidrow hadn't dragged me to her place and doctored me," Paxton said. He explained about being shot and taken to the house at the spring. "I've got to rest. That's the most exercise I've had since I walked up there."

Rooker helped him inside. "Now I want to know all the details, especially since you've been cooped up in that house with Loanda."

"Loanda didn't stay there much. I've only been on my feet three or four days."

"I'm surprised that Sam Tidrow didn't beef you," Rooker said.

"He didn't know I was there. I think someone got wise to it today. Ortis sneaked in, but I rigged up a bucket to fall when the door came open, and it dropped over his head. Made a good drum for my gun. He was pretty well subdued when I left."

Rooker grinned. "That makes one addle-brained gunman. But he'll be one mad gunman when he gets his brains unscrambled. Think he was the one who shot you?"

"I don't have any idea who it was. The man came down from the bluffs, but I played dead and I guess he thought I was."

"That's twice they've been sure they've killed you. They've got to believe you're a ghost now."

"Maybe," Paxton agreed. "But make-believe ghosts bleed like anybody else. What day is it?"

Rooker grinned. "Lost track of time while you were with Loanda, did you? We're starting the last week in September."

Paxton ignored Rooker's gibe. "That lawyer said my brother and I had until October 4 to claim our inheritance or we would lose it. That's not many days away."

"You and your brother have to be together to claim that land?"

"That's what the lawyer says. Uncle Josh

knew I wanted to see my brother sometime. This has to be his way of getting it done. I'm sure Gary is here at Monotony if I can just find him."

"They told me in town that he'd been here inquiring about you," Rooker said. "But nobody knows where he is now."

"I wish I could talk to the lawyer," Paxton said. "I wired him from Fort Hays that I was on my way here. I thought he would be here before this."

"I'll go to town and see if he's here," Rooker said. "I want you to keep out of sight now. Ghosts show up just on special occasions. It's the only way we're going to keep you alive, I think. Someone might be trying to kill your brother too."

"I've thought of that. If they kill one of us, the other one can't inherit that land alone. Might be the same man who is trying to kill me."

"Could be, but I doubt it. Norrid and Ortis being in that lynch mob says it's the Circle N after you. How could they know about your brother or Joshua's will leaving the spring to him and you?"

"They shouldn't know about that," Paxton agreed. "Josh may have said something about me but he wouldn't have mentioned Gary."

"There's a preacher on a homestead up north of here," Rooker said. "He was a good friend of Joshua Greer. Let's go up tonight and talk to him. He might have some answers for your questions."

Paxton agreed. Anything was better than sitting and doing nothing. He waited impatiently for darkness to settle down. Rooker had brought the extra horse up from the pasture, a raw-boned black horse that looked as if he had outlived his generation.

They left as soon as it was dark. As they rode, Rooker told him about Sutcliffe.

"Oscar Sutcliffe is a preacher of sorts. He has a church in Monotony. Preaches on Sunday, farms the rest of the time. I doubt if he's much of a preacher, but I've never heard him. He goes to town a lot, so he hears about everything that happens."

Oscar Sutcliffe was a rather heavy man with smoke-brown eyes and black hair. His solemn face gave him a dour look. Paxton didn't think he'd want to listen to him preach every Sunday.

"Joshua was a good man," Sutcliffe said in somber tones that fit his appearance. "But he was a stranger in a strange land. Few people understood him."

"Why would anybody kill him?" Paxton asked.

"I don't know," Sutcliffe said, "unless it was because he was in the way. The Circle N used that spring for a watering hole and Joshua fenced it off. Joshua said that was his personal property and the cattle could go downstream half a mile and get water."

"You blame Norrid for his death?" Paxton asked.

Sutcliffe held up his hand. "I blame no one. 'Judge not that ye be not judged.' I'm just reciting the facts. Whoever killed Joshua may have killed Roy Greer too. Both were holding the spring."

It was obvious that Sutcliffe thought the Circle N had been behind both murders. Paxton doubted if he knew that Joshua had been one of the train robbers. Paxton wondered why Josh had stayed if he'd found the money. But he remembered that Joshua was a stubborn man. Nobody could push him around.

"Anyway," Sutcliffe went on, "they burned the killer in that fire. You won't find him to vent your anger on."

"Think his spirit will return?" Rooker asked.

Sutcliffe's dark eyes blazed as if from a hidden fire. "Could be," he exclaimed with sudden animation. "Bertha had a dream that a spirit was going to bring a message for someone. Maybe it's for you from Joshua or Roy or maybe even the killer."

"When is this message coming through?" Rooker asked, his own eyes bright.

"She's having a seance in the grove outside town tomorrow night. Only the believers can be close to her, or the spirits won't speak. But anyone can stand off at a distance. If the message is for you, she'll call you."

"Won't be for me," Rooker said. "But it might be for Dave here. You'll be there, won't you?"

"You can be sure of that," Sutcliffe said. "I'll be right at Bertha's side. I want to know who killed my friend, Joshua."

"If you get to talk to any spirits, find out what has happened to a man named Gary Wirth. He was here just a few days ago and hasn't been seen lately," Paxton said.

Sutcliffe shook his head. "You can't force a spirit to reveal any information he doesn't think should be given out."

"Will Elias be there?" Rooker asked.

"Maybe," Sutcliffe said. "He is not a believer, but he wants to know everything we find out. Bertha is hoping to make a believer of him."

They left, Paxton entertaining doubts about Sutcliffe. He had never met anyone quite like him. He couldn't doubt his sincerity about the return of the spirits, but Paxton would doubt anything Sutcliffe told him they said. Paxton would have to classify himself with Elias Norrid — a doubter.

"I've got an idea," Rooker said as they reached the creek. "It's a wild one but it might scare somebody into telling the truth."

"What kind of an idea?"

"A ghost idea," Rooker said, grinning. "I'll tell you more if I can figure a way to make it work. I'm going to ride on into town tonight. You go on to my place and lay low. I mean, really lay low. Don't show a hair. Then tomorrow night as soon as it's dark, you ride Old Nig down the creek to the grove of cottonwoods. I'll meet you there."

He wheeled his horse and disappeared into the darkness before Paxton could ask him anything else about his scheme. Paxton didn't know whether this was a plan to get some information or just a practical joke. Rooker loved a good joke, he knew.

Going on to Rooker's place, he put the horse away and went inside. He was wondering what Rooker had in mind when he went to sleep.

Throughout most of the next day, he stayed inside the cavelike house, peering outside now and then. In the afternoon, restlessness drove him out to the barn where he got the old black horse and rode down the creek to the sod barn near the house where he had almost burned to death. That was right on his way to town, and he didn't want to be late in meeting Rooker.

Just as he reached the barn, he saw a rider coming from the northeast. Quickly, he turned his horse inside and stripped the saddle and bridle off him. Leading him back behind the hay stacked in the barn, he hurried around and pushed the hay away from the mouth of the tunnel. Then he watched as the rider came near. If he turned in, he'd crawl into the tunnel.

The rider came close to the sod barn but didn't stop. Paxton saw that it was the white-headed Elias Norrid. He wondered where he was going. Wherever it was, it could mean trouble for him.

Chapter 8

Elias Norrid rode close by the ashes of the old house that the mob had burned the other night. He got some satisfaction out of knowing that the man they had been chasing had died in that blaze. It wasn't safe for him to be running around.

As he approached the barn, he thought he caught a movement inside. He peered in through the openings that had once been doors, but he didn't see anything. It could be that a Circle N cow was inside eating some of the hay, although he didn't know why a cow would eat dry hay when there was still good grass to be had.

Glancing up at the sun, he rode on. He had to get to the Circle N, deliver his message and get back to town before dark. He was glad to get past the burned house. It was like riding past a graveyard, and he didn't like that at all. Maybe Bertha would like it. She seemed to thrive on spirits and ghosts.

There was something mysterious going

on along Cottonwood Creek that he couldn't quite understand. He didn't like that, either. He wanted to know everything that was going on and be in control of it. From what Sam Tidrow told him, there were even mysterious things happening up around the spring. It still irked him when he thought of the way Loanda had practically run him off the spring yesterday. Things like that simply couldn't be tolerated.

As he came in sight of the Circle N, he thought of Kucek. Why had he come back uninvited? Didn't he know that it wasn't safe to show his face around Monotony unless he was called in for a job? Well, he had paid the price. Being burned to death in a fire wasn't very pleasant, but if Kucek couldn't be trusted any further than that, he deserved to die. Norrid sighed. It was too bad though. He might have used Kucek again if what his lawyer told him about Joshua Greer's will was true.

Riding into the yard at the Circle N, he reined up and waited for Sam Tidrow to come from the corrals on the other side of the barn. He could have ridden down there, but it was Tidrow's place to come to him.

Tidrow, slim and trim at around a hundred and fifty pounds, came hurrying over from the corrals. Norrid frowned. It wasn't fair that some people could stay slim no matter how they enjoyed eating while others put on pounds just by looking at food. He heaved himself out of the saddle as the Circle N manager reached the horse.

"You didn't call Kucek back here for anything, did you?" Norrid asked.

Tidrow shook his head. "He must have come without being called. Didn't seem very smart of him to show up right in town like that."

"I didn't want to be seen at that lynching, but I didn't have a choice. Some people suspect me of hiring Kucek to kill Greer. Approving of his lynching should convince them I didn't."

"He deserved what he got," Tidrow said, "if he couldn't follow orders better than that."

"Kucek did his job well, and he got paid well. I might have had another job for him sometime if he'd used some sense."

"Maybe he had some other interest in the country," Tidrow said. "He asked a lot of questions when he was here the last time to kill Roy Greer."

"What kind of questions?" Norrid demanded, his snowy eyebrows squeezing together.

Tidrow shrugged. "Mostly about the spring. I just figured he wanted to know the lay of the land for sure before he tackled Greer. But maybe he had some other interest."

Norrid nodded slowly. "He should have remembered the lay of the land from the time before when he took care of Joshua. You don't suppose he had heard about the money they say is buried at that spring?"

"It's possible. He might have seen the same old newspaper you did and guessed this is the spring."

"If he knew, maybe some others know too," Norrid said, his brow furrowed in thought. "We'd better keep an eye on that spring."

"Loanda lives over there. What can happen while she's there?"

"Is she there now?"

Tidrow frowned. "Well, she's here today. I had a colt to start gentling, and she offered to do it."

Norrid scowled harder. He had thought he had things sewed up over at the spring when he put Loanda there. Maybe he was worse off than before. He'd been so sure everything was under control that he hadn't been watching it himself.

"She can't keep tabs on the spring very well from here, can she? Call her over here."

Tidrow turned to the barn and brought Loanda back.

"Been working with that yearling colt in the back corral," Loanda said as she came up. "You wanted to see me, Mr. Norrid?"

"I thought you were supposed to stay at the spring and make sure nobody else came there," Norrid said angrily.

"I'm there every night and part of the daytime," Loanda said. "Who's going to run off with the spring anyway?"

"I don't want anybody even to come there," Norrid snapped.

Loanda shook her head. "They can't drink all the water. And they can't take squatters rights. I'm doing that. So what's the difference whether I sit there all day or help Pa over here?"

Norrid knew she had him backed into a corner. It was unreasonable for him to expect her to stay right there all the time. He had told her he wanted her to stay there to keep other squatters off. Just living in the house would do that. Still, he was uneasy, and when he was uneasy, he could expect something to go wrong. Maybe he was just a bit psychic like Bertha. Not as much as

Bertha, thank goodness. But certain feelings seemed to precede trouble. Those feelings were stirring in him now.

"Are there any signs of anyone digging around the spring?" he asked.

Loanda nodded. "There are holes all around there like some aggravated badger had been at work."

"Who did the digging?"

"How do I know?" Loanda retorted. "Nobody left any calling cards."

"If you'd been there, you'd have known," Norrid snapped, letting his anger show.

"I don't sit up at night watching," Loanda shot back. "All the digging has been done at night. I didn't hear anybody, and I didn't see anybody."

Sam Tidrow stared at his daughter. "You may be in danger staying over there alone. You'd better stay here nights."

"She's staying over there," Norrid said sharply. "That was the bargain. Whoever is digging isn't thinking about bothering her, or he'd have done it before this."

"Let's go take a look," Tidrow suggested.

"Good idea," Norrid said. "We'll all go."

Loanda and her father went to the corral and roped out horses. While they saddled up, Norrid got back in the saddle. It wasn't easy any more for him to get on a horse. Sixty-two years weighted down by two hundred and ten pounds made mounting a horse anything but a simple chore.

As the two came from the corral, Norrid remembered the real reason he had come out here today. Bertha would peel his hide off if he forgot.

"Bertha is having a seance tonight at the grove just outside town," he said. "She wants you and as many of your hands as will come to be there."

"Me too?" Loanda asked.

"If you're set on coming," Norrid agreed. "But don't leave that spring too long, especially at night if that's when they're doing the digging."

"I'll be there," Tidrow said. "Bertha comes up with some weird shows. I wouldn't miss it. Reckon Vic and Al will come too. Maybe some of the others."

"Won't be any great show," Norrid muttered. "Just some moaning and groaning, then Bertha will tell everybody what she claims to have heard."

"She's been pretty accurate with her predictions," Tidrow said.

They cut across the three and a half miles to the spring. Loanda looked worried as they neared the house.

"My house is in no shape for company," she said.

"We're not company," Norrid snapped. "You're the company. It's my land."

"You said it was mine if I stayed on it."

Norrid nodded. He'd almost said the wrong thing. "Sure it is, because I'm giving it to you. I want you to stay there. I don't want to have to hire a man to clear the spring again."

"I hope you don't hire Kucek to get rid of me like you did Joshua and Roy Greer," Loanda said.

Norrid scowled and glared at Tidrow. He'd talked too much. Loanda knew more than any woman ought to know about men's business. "No danger of getting Kucek to do any more jobs," he said. "He's dead, remember."

They rode directly to the spring and slowly around it. Norrid stared in disbelief at the dozen or more holes dug around the perimeter of the spring. He heaved himself out of the saddle and got down to examine the holes. Some had been partially filled again but others were left open as if the digger didn't care who saw what he'd done. Most had been dug long ago.

"That one and that one," Norrid said, pointing, "are fresh. Too fresh for Kucek to be the one who dug them. Somebody else is looking."

"Don't see any pattern to the holes," Tidrow said. "Loanda, get a shovel."

"Have you got a gun, Loanda?" Norrid asked.

"Of course. And I know how to use it."

"Keep it handy from now on. Day or night, if you see anyone poking around out here at the spring, you use that gun. And shoot to kill."

Loanda went on toward the house to get a shovel as if she hadn't heard him. Norrid felt his face flush. If she got uppity with him, he'd throw her off the spring and put someone out here he could trust. She needn't think she owned this land yet.

With the shovel, Tidrow dug several holes in the vicinity of the others. The shovel hit nothing harder than some gravel in a spot or two. Loanda watched for a while then announced that she was going to the house. That was fine with Norrid. He had some things to talk over with Tidrow. He didn't need any extra ears.

"We'll have to have a map or some guide to show us where to dig," Tidrow said, leaning on the shovel.

"Looks like it," Norrid agreed. "If there

is any gold, I'll give you a share if you find it."

"I was wondering if Kucek did know about Joshua's gold," Tidrow said. "That would explain why he was handy when we needed him to do away with the old man. And he seemed plenty willing to kill him and Roy too. Maybe he was the one doing the digging."

"Not those last holes," Norrid said. "He was burned in that old house. No ghost dug those holes."

"Reckon that's right. Somebody else knows about Joshua's gold. Maybe we shouldn't have been in such a hurry to get rid of Kucek. We might have had another job for him."

Norrid nodded. "I was thinking the same. But we had to make a good appearance in town. They recognized him. If I hadn't agreed to lynching him, they'd have said I wanted him to go free. Couldn't have that. Anyway, he was a threat to us. Can you imagine what would have happened if he'd had a chance to blow his horn about us?"

"Funny he didn't try to say something when our boys were about to hang him. Do you suppose that wasn't Kucek?"

That panicky feeling flitted through

Norrid's stomach again. He'd had it a time or two when he looked right at the man before they started to hang him. Something about him was different — as if he weren't really Kucek.

"Old Josh Greer threatened once to send for his nephew, Dave Paxton, who he said was a fast gun," Norrid said. "My lawyer says he heard that Paxton might inherit this land from Greer. If that wasn't Kucek we burned, maybe it was Paxton?"

"In that case, we're lucky to have gotten rid of him anyway," Tidrow said. "We don't need another Greer relative on this spring, especially if he's a fast man with a gun."

"Not likely that another man could look so much like Kucek," Norrid said, trying to convince himself they had burned the right man. "A man we must watch is that squatter's son, Jeff Rooker. He and Roy Greer were pretty chummy. He's still around, ain't he?"

Tidrow nodded. "He's hanging out in Seaton's old dugout. I don't take him for much of a gunfighter. We can handle him. If he starts showing his spurs, I'll turn Vic Ortis loose on him."

Norrid jumped as he heard a sound over the knoll to the east beyond the spring. He looked that way but didn't see anything. He wheeled on Tidrow.

"Did you hear anything?"

"Thought I did," Tidrow said. "Let's ride over and see."

By the time Norrid pulled his hulk up into the saddle, he found himself several jumps behind Tidrow. Norrid flogged his horse into a run.

Just as his horse hit a gallop, he saw a rider on a black horse topping a knoll a quarter of a mile away. It looked like Kucek — or the man they had tried to hang and finally had burned. He shook his head. He'd been listening to his sister, Bertha, too much. Now he was seeing ghosts. Maybe they could catch this one and see if he would bleed.

Chapter 9

Dave Paxton kicked the old black horse into his fastest gallop which seemed agonizingly slow to a man in a hurry. It was a mile to Rooker's and almost as far beyond that to the sod barn. He doubted if the old black horse could keep ahead of Tidrow and Norrid that far.

The two pursuers were gaining rapidly. Paxton headed for a high ridge. At the top, he reined to the left and followed the ridge a ways then cut down off it. In the valley, he turned back sharply to the right and over another smaller ridge, getting out of sight before the pursuers could top the big ridge.

He wasn't sure that would delay Tidrow and Norrid. If it didn't they would catch up with him sooner than if he'd held a straight course. But if his ruse threw them off, even for a couple of minutes, that might give him enough time to get to that tunnel between the old sod barn and the burned house.

Turning the old horse downstream along the bank of the creek, he pushed him to his top speed which wasn't nearly equal to Paxton's demands. He thought of Rooker and his admonition to stay indoors where no one would see him. It had been good advice, but something about Norrid riding toward the Circle N had nudged him into following to find out what he had in mind.

He hadn't been close enough to hear what was being said, but their actions at the spring had told him a lot. Even from a distance, Norrid's excitement when he saw the holes around the spring told Paxton that he was afraid someone had found the money that Joshua Greer had supposedly been looking for. Up until that moment, Paxton hadn't thought that anybody else had known about the money. But Norrid and Tidrow knew. Somebody else did too, or there wouldn't have been all those holes around the spring. Maybe those holes had been dug by Roy trying to find the money.

Glancing back as he passed Rooker's place, Paxton saw that the two riders were just now turning his way from the big ridge. He had gained considerable distance, enough, he hoped, that he would be able to reach the sod barn and disappear into that tunnel without leaving any trace of where he went.

He urged the old horse on relentlessly. The horse was willing, but the vigor to power that willingness was just about gone.

As he neared the barn, he watched his pursuers. When they disappeared behind a knoll, he dropped into a gully and stopped the horse. He leaped off, headed the horse up the gully and gave him a slap. He knew he wouldn't go far without anyone to urge him on.

Bending low, Paxton ran hard toward the sod barn, ducking inside without catching sight of the two riders behind him. He ran to the tunnel mouth and pulled the hay away. Crawling inside, he pulled the hay back over the mouth of the tunnel. Then he backed a few feet away from the end of the tunnel and waited. From here, he would hear what went on inside the barn. But he'd still be far enough back that, if they did uncover the tunnel mouth, they wouldn't see him as soon as he'd see them.

He didn't have long to wait till he heard sounds in the barn. He held his gun in his hand while he waited, ears strained to hear what was going on. Caution apparently was forcing the men to move slowly.

"I didn't see him riding beyond the

barn," a man said finally. "He must have stopped here."

"I thought I saw something in here as I was coming out to the ranch today," the other man said.

Paxton identified the voices then. That last one would have to be Norrid so the other one must be Tidrow.

"Sure don't see nothing in here now," Tidrow said. "Hey, look here behind this pile of hay. A horse has been here."

"No horse here now," Norrid said. "That fellow must not have stopped here like we thought."

"Looks like we'll have to let him go."

"Can't do that," Norrid said quickly. "If he saw us digging, he may guess what we were digging for. Too many people know about that already. We've got to find him."

"All right," Tidrow said irritably. "Go ahead and find him if you can."

"He must have turned up one of those gullies that run back from the creek. We're wasting time here."

Paxton stayed in the tunnel as the sounds died away outside. They would find the old black horse saddled and bridled and they'd know he wasn't too far away. After failing to find him in the barn, they'd likely scour the hills and bluffs along the creek. Paxton had to stay out of sight.

He had no way of guessing what time it was, so after a long wait, he moved to the end of the tunnel and pushed a little of the hay aside. It was twilight. Shoving the hay away, he crawled out into the barn and put the hay back over the tunnel mouth. He stepped to the doorway and looked out. There was no sign of Norrid and Tidrow.

Going outside, he looked around for his black horse. Tidrow might have taken him back to the Circle N, but it wasn't likely he'd want a bony old horse like that. He soon spotted the old black up the gully where he had sent him earlier this afternoon.

He moved out of the barn and up the gully to the old horse. The horse lifted his head but didn't move when he came up. Mounting, he nudged the horse into reluctant motion. He wouldn't ask him to run again if he didn't have to.

It was well past dark when he approached the grove of cottonwoods just above town. It had been at the lone cottonwood behind the blacksmith shop just below the grove that they'd tried to hang him. There were little fires spotted here and there over the grove and as he drew closer, he saw people bunched around the blazes.

Down near the center of the grove was a bigger fire that seemed to be set well apart from the rest. That would be where Bertha was holding her seance, Paxton guessed.

As he reached the end of the grove, Rooker stepped out from a tree and flagged him down.

"Thought you were never going to make it," he said softly.

"You said to wait till dark," Paxton countered.

Rooker nodded. "I've spread the word that the ghost of the gunfighter they burned in the homesteader's cabin is loose on the creek." His grin was visible in the dim light. "They're jumpy as a bunch of pin-stuck frogs."

"Who do you mean by they?"

"Everybody. Maybe Bertha ain't. This is her show, and she's so sure she can handle everything. But most of these people waiting around here are the ones who half believe in what she's doing. They're skittish, not sure what to expect."

"Are you figuring on having the ghost show up?"

Rooker laughed softly. "Sure am. You're it. Come here."

Paxton followed Rooker into the trees. He stopped, staring in disbelief. He saw the pure white horse first. Then he saw the long white coat and the white hat.

"That's the ghost?" he asked.

"It will be, as soon as you get in those duds and on that horse. You'll ride without a saddle. Want everything white. Shows up better at night. We'll make believers of these people."

"Believers in what?" Paxton asked. "What will we gain?"

"I ain't sure yet, but we ain't got nothing to lose. That's Bertha and her bevy of believers down there in the middle of the grove. There ain't much underbrush. People from town have gathered it all for firewood. So you can ride free under the trees. Start out by swinging up on the other bank of the creek. People will see you there. Then swing down through the trees."

"I'll probably get shot."

"Nobody's going to shoot a ghost. At least, not these people. They already half believe in spirits. It would be horrible luck if they hurt one."

"Would be for me, all right," Paxton agreed.

The fire in the center of the grove blazed a little higher and sounds of an incantation flowed through the grove.

"She's at it," Rooker whispered. "Listen close as she calls on the spirits."

Paxton listened and was surprised at the absolute quiet that reigned over the grove. Then Bertha's voice rose to a higher pitch as she announced that the spirits were coming.

"That's your cue," Rooker said. "Get going."

Against his better judgment, Paxton donned the long white coat and big white hat then mounted the horse. The horse sidestepped warily.

"He's a bit skittish," Rooker said. "Hasn't been ridden lately. But you can handle him. Get going."

Paxton reined the horse to the far side of the grove and out to the top of the first rise above the creek bank. He was a fourth of the way along the length of the grove when a scream from one of the closer fires drew attention to him.

Paxton had seen panic before but nothing to top this. Screams echoed over the grove as heads pivoted toward him. What little light came from the stars and the fires reflected off the white and Paxton could guess that he must look something like a ghost rider floating along above the creek.

Getting into the spirit of the thing, he reined the horse down toward the grove. Just a ghost rider wouldn't be enough to convince people unless they saw the face of the rider. Already half believing that the ghost of the gunfighter was on the prowl, there would be no doubt left in the mind of anyone who got a look at Paxton's face.

As Paxton entered the trees, a man suddenly burst out from behind a tree almost directly in his path. Paxton saw the shock of white hair and realized that it was Elias Norrid. Norrid apparently had wanted to see what was going on but didn't want Bertha to know that he would stoop to coming to her seance.

Paxton had to jerk on the reins to keep the horse from hitting Norrid. Norrid threw up his arms and screamed, "Kucek!"

The horse, already skittish, wheeled and grabbed the bit in his teeth, breaking into a run straight across the grove. Paxton, riding bareback, had to hang on and duck low to keep branches from sweeping him off the horse.

The horse was heading directly for Bertha's inner circle and Paxton had no way of changing his course. Norrid, behind him now, was screaming at Bertha to run. Bertha had had her back to Paxton and had refused to come out of her trance to notice earthly things around her. But now she wheeled to face the charging white horse.

"The spirit is coming!" she shouted more in elation than fear.

It was the first time Paxton had seen Bertha. Her two hundred and forty pound frame would have been awesome under most circumstances, but it looked no more formidable than a tumbleweed before the charging horse.

Someone grabbed Bertha and jerked her back against a tree. Paxton recognized Oscar Sutcliffe as he leaped high, grabbing a tree limb and pulling himself up out of the way of the horse. The crowd around the fire that had been entranced by Bertha only a moment before was scattering now like an exploding firecracker.

As Paxton flashed past the fire and under the tree where Sutcliffe had taken refuge, he felt the urge to enter into the spirit of the occasion. He yelled shrilly: "Death to the killers!"

As he dashed past the tree, he saw Sutcliffe lose his grip and come crashing down. But he didn't hit the ground. He landed directly on top of Bertha. It was a soft landing for Sutcliffe, but if Bertha still felt that she was in a trance, that would jar her out of it.

The horse charged on, coming out of the trees on the town side of the grove. The slope toward town was covered with running, screaming people. An earthquake couldn't have evoked any more terror than the appearance of the white horse and rider at the moment when Bertha was announcing the arrival of the spirits.

Once out of the trees, Paxton gained some control of the white horse. He no longer had to keep his head down to avoid branches and he sawed on the reins until he had the horse headed back toward the upper end of the grove where Rooker should be waiting.

He expected someone to shoot at him, out of pure fright if for no other reason. But no shot came, and he was leaving the terrified people behind with every leap of the horse. The seance was over. The scene was unreal enough to make Paxton feel almost like a ghost except that riding this horse bareback was not the way he would imagine a ghost would float through the air.

Chapter 10

At the edge of the grove, Paxton sawed the horse to a stop. At first, he thought that Rooker was gone, but then he heard him laughing. Dismounting, he found the little man leaning against a tree, holding his sides.

"That is . . . the funniest circus . . . I ever saw," he panted, gasping for breath.

"Maybe it wouldn't have been so funny if you'd been trying to stick on the slick back of this maniac running like a scared coyote under those trees," Paxton growled.

"Did you hear Bertha yelling after she got Sutcliffe off her lap?" Rooker puffed. "She said that was the most dramatic appearance of any spirit she ever called up."

"She thinks she called up me and this white thunderbolt?" Paxton demanded.

"She sure does. At least, she's going to take credit for it. Now you get that horse on up the creek. I'll be along just as soon as I catch my breath. If they see you now, they'll think they're still seeing the ghost."

"Some of them with a little more sense

will figure out that no ghost is going to tear through a grove of trees hanging on for dear life like I did."

"They weren't paying any attention to how you were hanging on. They were just hoping they could hang onto their scalps and their gizzards till they could get out of there themselves. Boy, what a show!" Rooker doubled over with laughter again.

Paxton reined the white horse up the creek and loosened the reins. The horse was far from run down. He hit full stride in two jumps and thundered up the bank of the creek. A few wild screams from back toward town proved that some people had seen him and were still frightened out of their wits.

Paxton let the horse run until he was ready to slow down. Then, in a ravine running down to the creek halfway between town and Rooker's dugout, he reined up to wait.

It was a half hour before Rooker arrived, riding his horse and leading the old black. Paxton heard him chuckling before he reined to a halt.

"If I live to be a thousand, I won't forget that seance," Rooker said.

"Reckon there are some others who may remember it for a while too," Paxton said, "including me."

"You should have seen them scatter after you left me. Some of them saw you, and the panic started all over again for those who hadn't already made it back to town. They were squealing like stuck pigs." Rooker broke into laughter again.

"Wish I thought it was as funny as you do," Paxton said.

"You didn't see it from where I did," Rooker said, taking a deep breath and curbing his laughter. "I stuck around long enough to find out how things turned out. Bertha is a powerful force in Monotony now. She takes the credit for bringing you to life, and there ain't nobody willing to argue with her. They saw you and not one of them can give a logical argument to prove that you weren't a ghost. That includes Elias Norrid. He was shaking like a leaf in a tornado and babbling like a stuttering monkey." He broke into laughter again.

"I don't see how this is going to be of any help to me," Paxton said.

"Oh, it will," Rooker said. "Bertha's got the whole town thinking there are spirits and ghosts roaming around. Did you ever hear of anyone killing a ghost? They ain't likely to try killing you if they think you are a ghost. They'd try it quick enough if they thought you were real."

"Did Bertha get the message from the spirits she was expecting?"

Rooker chuckled. "I reckon you were message enough for all concerned. Most of those who were there are probably home hiding under the bed now. Of course, Tidrow and his two gun hands were there. They were still in town when I left. They should be riding along this way pretty quick." He glanced at the moon just rising. "Maybe we ought to give them something else to think about."

Paxton frowned. "Such as?"

"That white outfit on a white horse ought to show up pretty well in the moonlight if you were up on the bluff."

Paxton nodded, catching some of Rooker's enthusiasm. "If I'm going to play ghost again, I'd better get up there."

"Those three were in the mob that tried to burn you alive. So you owe them something. This will be one installment."

Paxton nodded and mounted the white horse again. He didn't like riding bareback but he didn't have time to switch his saddle over from the black. Heading up a gully that led toward the top of the bluff, he urged the white horse on. This horse was a real contrast to Rooker's old black he'd been riding. This one was young and full of fire. He climbed the ravine eagerly, breaking out on top of the bluff in a trot.

Angling back to the lip of the bluff overlooking the valley, Paxton stopped the white horse and waited. In less than five minutes, he saw three riders coming up the river road. That would be Tidrow and Al Zamora and Vic Ortis. Rooker had said Tidrow had his two gun hands along. Paxton did owe them something.

He pulled his horse back from the bluff's edge and stopped where he could just see the riders approaching. When they were almost even with him, he nudged his horse into a gallop along the edge of the bluff, giving vent to a yell he'd used as a kid playing Indians.

Down below the three riders yanked back on their reins, one horse rearing from the sudden jerk. They stared up at the top of the bluff. Then, as if they were of one body and mind, all three slapped their horses with their hats and spurs and reined straight across the creek. They headed directly toward the Circle N, going where no trail had ever gone before.

Before Paxton got back to the river bottom, he heard Rooker laughing again. This had been a great evening for him.

Paxton saw some of the humor now.

"Wish you could have seen them up close," Rooker said when Paxton reached him. "You picked the right time to give that yell. They were right out there not twenty yards from me. I'll swear one of them was bawling like a baby when he rode out of here. He was so scared he couldn't have run a step if he'd been afoot. Bet he won't ever ride this trail again after dark."

"Ready to go home now?"

"I reckon. But you missed part of the show. Right behind the Circle N boys was Oscar Sutcliffe. I'd forgotten about him. He went whooping past me like his shirttail was on fire and he had a tailwind. He was screaming something about not being ready to go yet. But he was going, just the same."

They started home, Rooker still convulsed on occasion as he thought over what he had seen. Paxton was enjoying it now, catching the humor of it from Rooker. It would have been a lot funnier if he hadn't been a participant. Sitting on the sidelines, Rooker had enjoyed the whole show.

"Enough of them saw your face to prove beyond doubt that it was the ghost of the gunfighter they had killed," Rooker said after he'd stopped chuckling. "They'll have due respect for you wherever and whenever they see you now."

"Where did you get this horse?" Paxton asked, thinking he might need it again. It was certainly better than the old black crowbait.

"That's one of the Circle N horses," Rooker said, grinning. "They've got about a dozen pure white horses that they run on the lower Cottonwood. I just borrowed one."

"We'd better put him back before they miss him."

"They don't check that herd often. Nobody would steal one because those white horses are known all over the country."

"Then we don't want to get caught with one."

"That ain't no ordinary horse now," Rooker said, chuckling again. "He's a ghost horse. We'll take him back to that sod barn where you were almost burned. Hide him back of that pile of hay. If it looks like they might find him there, turn him loose. He'll go back to his pasture, and no one will be the wiser."

"Don't they ride these white horses much?"

Rooker shook his head. "They're all

broke to ride, but they're Norrid's hobby. Almost like show horses. They wouldn't be much good on the business end of a rope. Since they ain't used much, they get pretty skittish."

"You don't have to tell me that," Paxton said. "For a high-strung critter, he's sure got a tough mouth."

They reached the sod barn and Paxton reined up. "I'll just stay here the rest of the night," he said. "I'm going to Monotony tomorrow. My brother must be there somewhere, and I've got to find him."

"That would be a fool thing to do," Rooker said. "Making people believe you're a ghost will keep you alive if you play it smart. But if you go riding into town where they can see you're alive and kicking, then somebody is going to start gunning for you again."

"That lawyer's letter said we had till October 4 to claim our inheritance. I don't know how much that might mean to my brother. I've got to find him."

"You sure are asking to be killed," Rooker said, no trace of the laughter of the last hour in his voice.

"I've got to do something. Doing nothing will lose that land just as sure as if I was dead."

Rooker sighed. "I reckon nothing I can say will stop you. So you'd better find out what you can in a hurry. There's a loafer in town called Icky Minton. He's not too bright. His name is Mickey but when he's drunk, and that's most of the time, he calls himself Icky. You look him up. If he's half-sober he can tell you everything that's going on in town. All he does is watch and listen and drink. He won't talk unless you give him some money or another bottle. For a bottle of whiskey, he'd tell a killer where his mother was hiding."

"Where will I find this Icky?"

"In the pool hall. That's the only place in town where he can get his liquid amnesia."

"I'll look him up," Paxton promised as he swung off his horse.

Rooker handed him the reins of the black horse. "Don't ride that white one to town. And don't expect to find Icky before ten o'clock. That's when the pool hall opens."

"I'll let you know what I find out," Paxton promised.

"I hope so," Rooker muttered as he nudged his horse on toward his place.

Paxton fretted through the early hours next morning at the barn, not wanting to get to Monotony until he was sure he could find Icky Minton quickly. He wasn't minimizing his chances of getting shot. But he'd waited long enough for someone else to bring him word of Gary Wirth. If Gary was in Monotony, he was going to find him.

Wearing his dark clothes and riding the old black horse, Paxton started to town about half past nine. He figured Icky would be at the pool hall by the time he got there.

He pulled his hat low over his face and rode slumped in the saddle like a trail-weary cowboy as he came into the street. He had intended to tie at the hitchrack in front of the pool hall but he changed his mind. The deputy, Tug Buskey, was slumped in a chair tipped back against the front of the pool hall.

Riding on to the store next door, he pulled up and dismounted, keeping his back to the deputy. He wondered how he was going to get to Icky Minton if he was in the pool hall and the deputy was out front. Crossing the porch, he stepped inside the store. Only the owner, Quinton Upshaw, was in sight.

Upshaw, of medium height and far above medium weight, squinted at Paxton as he came in. Then recognition flooded his face, and he backed off a step.

"Where can I find Icky Minton?" Paxton demanded.

"Over in the pool hall, I reckon," Upshaw said, his lips trembling. "Where did you come from?"

Paxton saw the fear in his face and decided to add to it. "Where do ghosts usually come from?"

At the word ghost, Upshaw backed against the shelf behind him. His hand began inching toward the gun Paxton could see on the shelf.

Paxton forced a grin. "Do you think you can shoot a ghost?"

What was left of Upshaw's courage shattered, and he wheeled with a smothered gurgle and waddled at top speed toward the back door. The last Paxton saw of him through the door he left open, he was charging across the alley behind the store.

Paxton turned back toward the front just in time to see the deputy walk slowly past the store in the direction of the hotel, a block away. Paxton moved up to the front window to watch him. This was the break he was waiting for.

Buskey went past the bank and the lawyer's office. Paxton didn't wait to see if he was going to turn in at the hotel. Stepping out-side, he moved quickly to the front of the pool hall.

Bracing himself, he stepped to the door. What would he find inside? Would he meet a bullet? Not everyone would be as spooky as Upshaw had been. He might as well find out. Pushing open the door, he stepped in-side.

Chapter 11

It was darker inside the pool hall than it had
been inside the store. Paxton tried to see
every face in the room in the first sweep. His
eyes stopped momentarily on one man he
hadn't expected to see. Al Zamora, one of
the Circle N riders with Tidrow last night,
was sitting in a chair not far from one of the
pool tables. He had a bottle on the table
within arm's reach.

Zamora's eyes popped wide open when
he saw Paxton. Paxton expected him to
reach for his gun, but he seemed too startled to move.

Paxton's eyes ran over the others in the
room. There were only two. One appeared
to be in charge of the place, and there was
a man in his late thirties slouched in a
chair beside a table on the other side of the
pool tables. There was an almost empty
bottle sitting in front of him.

Paxton checked Zamora again, but he
was still just sitting there, the color gradually
coming back into his face. Then he looked

back at the other man. That must be Icky Minton. He had watery gray eyes and sandy hair that looked as if it hadn't ever been combed with anything but fingers. He was a small man with dirty clothes. Except for his disheveled look, he could disappear in a crowd and never be noticed. Paxton started toward the man, but Zamora was almost in the way.

The cowboy pushed his chair back. "You — you ain't Kucek," he stammered.

Paxton could hear the fear cracking his voice. He had to play on that fear or test Zamora's skill with a gun. Right now he just wanted to talk to Icky Minton.

"Did you think a ghost would look exactly like the man he was while he was still alive?"

Zamora got to his feet and backed behind the table. "You ain't no ghost."

"Want to bet on that?"

"I saw the ghost last night," Zamora said, confidence coming into his face.

"Twice," Paxton said. "Once in the grove and again out on the bluff. Were you the one who was bawling like a baby while he ran?"

That was too much for Zamora. He might not be fully convinced this was the ghost of Felix Kucek, but he knew that nobody but the ghost could possibly know that he had seen him twice last night or that one of the three Circle N men was so scared that he cried.

"Want to argue about it?" Paxton pressed.

Zamora was back against the wall, and he shook his head vigorously, his eyes fairly bulging out of his face.

Paxton turned to Icky. "I want to see you, Icky."

Icky Minton had pushed his bottle and glass back and gotten to his feet while Paxton was convincing Zamora that he was really the ghost. Now when Paxton turned his attention on Icky, the small man exploded into action, rushing toward the back door.

"Hold on, Icky," Paxton called.

But he was wasting his breath. The little man hit the back door with the force of an angry bull and popped it open. He disappeared into the alley. Paxton started after him then changed his mind. There was no telling how long the paralysis that was gripping Zamora would hold. Maybe no longer than the moment Paxton's back was turned.

Quickly backing toward the front door, he ducked outside and over to the alley between the pool hall and the general store.

Running down the alley, he broke into the wider alley that ran behind the business houses. He stumbled over piles of boxes and pieces of boards left over from some repair job on one of the buildings.

He stopped and looked up and down the rear of the buildings. He saw Icky across the side street to his right running down the alley as if he had truly seen a ghost.

Glancing at the rear door of the pool hall to make sure that Zamora wasn't there, he turned toward Icky. It was obvious to Paxton that Icky wasn't drunk now. If he had been drunk in the pool hall, he had sobered up very quickly. No man even tipsy could run like Icky was doing now.

Paxton was no great foot racer, but he thought he could hold his own with a small man like Icky Minton. However, he was being outdistanced with every step.

He crossed the side street and went behind the bank. He glanced to his left when he caught a movement off in the distance. He saw Quinton Upshaw, the storekeeper, puffing up the slope to the second bench above the creek. A huge house sat on that level and, even from this distance, Paxton could see the big Circle N burned into the log over the gateway. That would be the house where Elias Norrid lived. Upshaw must live along that street somewhere.

Pushing Upshaw out of his mind, he turned back to his pursuit of Icky. He was just in time to see Icky duck into a stairway leading down to a cellar under the hotel.

Paxton ran to the stairs and looked down. There was a door opening off the stairway into a room under the hotel. Icky had to be there. But would he have a gun and start shooting the instant Paxton showed up? He had to take that chance. Rooker had said Icky would know more about what was going on in town than anyone else.

His best chance of preventing Icky from shooting at him was to strike quickly. The longer Icky had to prepare for Paxton's coming, the more likely he was to think of some way to defend himself.

Paxton bounded down the steps two at a time. At the bottom, he whirled toward the door and threw a shoulder against it. It yielded with a bang and Paxton found himself in a small room, crowded with broken furniture, piles of rags and clothes, and dirty dishes.

Icky Minton was cowering at the far side of the room, looking as harmless as a frightened pup. Paxton stopped, thinking that he had no right to barge in on Icky and scare the life out of him this way. There were disadvantages as well as advantages to the ghost image Rooker had helped him create.

"I just wanted to ask you some questions, Icky," Paxton said softly.

"I — I ain't got nothing to say to a — a ghost," Icky chattered.

"Maybe I'm not a ghost."

"Yes, you are," Icky said positively. "Al recognized you. He ain't scared of no man but he's sure scared of you."

Paxton guessed that Icky was no mental genius, drunk or sober. That still wouldn't prohibit him from hearing and remembering all the things that were being said and done around him.

"Look at me, Icky," Paxton said. "I'm not going to hurt you. I'm going to stay over here by the door. Is this where you live?"

Icky nodded, his eyes watching every move that Paxton made, staring at his face as if to anticipate any danger that might be telegraphed from there.

"I work around the hotel," he said finally. "Keep the yard clean, carry in wood and water and carry out ashes. They give me this room to live in. I can eat at their table."

"That's a pretty good deal," Paxton said.

Icky's face lost some of its fear. "Sure is. I do the same work for the pool hall and Gus gives me some drinks. I wouldn't trade places with nobody."

Except for clothes, Icky had about everything he needed. Likely his clothes were those discarded by others. From the fit of the shirt he was wearing, Paxton would guess it hadn't been bought or made for him.

"Could you use some extra money, Icky? I need some information."

Icky's eyes brightened. "Sure could. I don't earn enough drinks over at the pool hall to get all I want."

Paxton took out a half dollar and laid it on the box that Icky obviously used for a table. "Ever see a man around named Gary Wirth?"

Icky stared at him, fear twisting his face again. There must be something about the name Wirth that frightened him. "I ain't seen him for a long time," he said.

Paxton was sure that he knew more than he was going to tell about Wirth. His eyes ran over the cluttered room and stopped on the sill of the little window that opened out on the stairwell. The window let in only a little light, but there were a dozen pocketknives on the sill.

"Do you like pocketknives?"

The fear subsided in Icky's face. "I sure do." He moved over to the window and fondled a couple of the knives, not pulling out the blades.

Paxton took out the pocketknife he carried. "If I gave you this knife, would you tell me about Wirth?"

Icky's eyes fastened on Paxton's knife like an eagle beaming in on a rabbit. "That's sure a pretty knife," he said, his breath coming in quick gasps.

"It will be yours if you'll talk to me," Paxton said.

Icky nodded eagerly, never taking his eyes off the knife.

Paxton kept the knife in his hand but out where Icky could see it. "Why are you afraid of me?" he asked.

"I know who you are. You're Felix Kucek. You killed Roy Greer then left the country."

"I'm not Kucek," Paxton said. "I wouldn't come back here if I'd killed somebody."

"Don't make sense," Icky admitted, "but you're Kucek, all right. I recognized you when you first came back. I saw Tug Buskey put you in jail, and I saw them break you out. Then I saw them try to

130

hang you, but you got away. Then you were caught in that house and burned to death. That's why I know you're a ghost, and I'm afraid of ghosts."

The terror was creeping back into his face and voice. Paxton had to reverse that trend or he would never find out anything.

"You don't have to be afraid of this ghost," he said softly. He handed the knife to Icky, and the terror faded from his face. "Who was Kucek?"

"A gunfighter," Icky said. "A good one too. I saw him beat a gambler down in the pool hall. Somebody hired him to kill Roy Greer."

"Do you know who hired him?"

Icky shook his head.

"Why did they have Roy killed?"

"Maybe because the Circle N needed the water in the spring. Tidrow talked about getting rid of Greer so he could have the water."

"Did Tidrow hire Kucek to kill Greer?"

Icky shook his head. "Maybe Mr. Norrid did. The Circle N is his. Tidrow does whatever Mr. Norrid tells him to."

Paxton was revising upward his estimate of Icky's mentality. Rooker was right about Icky knowing what was going on. Now if he would just tell him where Gary Wirth was!

"Have you seen Gary Wirth in town?" he asked.

Fear flashed across Icky's face again. His eyes fell on the knife in his hands, then he looked up at Paxton. "He was here asking for a man named Paxton. Then he went away, and I haven't seen him since."

"Did he leave town?"

"I don't think so."

"Could you find him?"

Icky frowned. "I ain't sure."

"Will you look for him?" Paxton asked.

Icky shrank back against the wall. "I might get beaten up or killed if I did."

"Who'd do that?"

Icky shook his head. "I don't know. But I know I shouldn't look."

"Was Wirth scared when you saw him?"

Icky nodded. "He was running from somebody but looking for Paxton."

Paxton frowned. He wasn't getting anywhere and wouldn't unless he could convince Icky to help him.

"I'll get you another pocketknife if you'll help me find Wirth," he said.

The battle between fear and the desire for another knife was acted out in Icky's face like the scenes of a play. Finally he gritted his teeth and looked up at Paxton.

"All right. If you'll get me a good knife,

I'll show you where I think he is."

Paxton had to settle for that. They went out the door and up the steps to the level of the alley. Icky stopped there, looking over at the back of the lawyer's office.

"Down there, I think," he said and turned and dived down the steps like a startled prairie dog.

Paxton started toward the lawyer's office, wondering what he would find when he got there.

Chapter 12

Gary Wirth saw the man over at the top of the cellar steps with Icky Minton. Warily he watched them. He'd had the feeling for some time that Icky knew he was hiding here in the back room of the lawyer's office, but for some reason he was afraid to come near the place. Now he and this stranger were looking over this way.

Then Icky dived back down the steps and the stranger moved slowly toward the lawyer's office. Gary slammed the bolt home on the inside of the rear door of the office. Lawyer Mark Horn apparently had never had a lock on this door although he did have one on the front door. Gary had gotten into this back room through the unlocked door. About the first thing he did was rig up a lock on the inside of the door from scraps he found here and at night over behind the blacksmith shop. He intended to use the lock only in an emergency. This looked like one to him.

He had never seen this man before.

Maybe it was someone he would like to know, and maybe it wasn't. So far, the few men he had met here were not ones he wanted to know. This man might be a gun-fighter hired by Caleb Yount to search him out and kill him. Gary couldn't take a chance.

He slipped through the partition door into the front office which looked like a lawyer's office instead of the junk shop that was the back room. Gary would have stayed in this room more, but he was afraid someone passing along the street outside might hear him moving around in there or maybe see a shadow through the thin curtains. He couldn't take that chance.

The man came to the back door cautiously as if expecting trouble. Gary was sure now that he must have been hired by Yount to kill him. Gary was no fighter. He wished he could handle a gun like his brother, Dave Paxton, could. He hadn't seen Dave since they were two and four years old but he'd had letters from him. Dave had said he had hired out his gun more than once in range wars, so he had to be mighty handy with a gun.

The man reached the door and tried to open it. Gary thanked his stars that he'd had foresight enough to put that bolt on the door. No one who didn't know Horn well would think anything of finding the back door of his office locked.

After peeking through the window awhile, the man turned and left. Gary came stealthily back into the rear room and closed the partition door. He felt safe again, as safe as he could feel here in Monotony.

He had considered trying to sneak out of town some night and going back to Texas where he could draw a free breath and not wonder what moment he was going to be killed.

He knew his chances of getting away without Yount beating him up again were slim. Besides, this was his chance to own some land. He had never owned anything of value before. There was another nagging thought too. What if his brother was depending on him to help inherit that land?

It was only because of his brother that Joshua Greer had willed Dave and him that land. Joshua hadn't known Gary. Evidently, Dave had wanted to be reunited with Gary and Joshua knew it, so he had made the provision in his will that he and Dave could inherit the land only if they appeared together. He wondered if Dave would have been given the land if it hadn't been for the added incentive of getting the brothers together.

Gary had wanted to see Dave ever since he was big enough to know he had a brother. He still recalled the thrill he'd gotten when that letter from Dave came to him in the Texas town where the Wirths had lived shortly after they had adopted Gary. From then on, he and his brother had corresponded, even though it was infrequently.

Then the letter had come from Mark Horn, the lawyer in Omaha, saying that he and Dave Paxton had inherited a quarter of land on Cottonwood Creek in Nebraska but that they would have to appear together to claim it. Gary had left immediately for Nebraska, sure that the lawyer would notify Dave, and he would be here to meet him.

When he got here, however, he didn't find Dave. He found Caleb Yount. Yount was a big man, weighing over two hundred pounds. And that weight was all muscle and meanness. He had turned that muscle and meanness on Gary the first time they met and had driven Gary into hiding.

Yount had warned him to get out of the country or worse things would happen to him. But Gary had come all the way from Texas to meet the brother he hadn't seen since he was two years old, and he wasn't going to give up without making more of an effort than he had already made to find him.

It was late September now. He had hoped to find Dave before this so they could claim the land Joshua Greer had left them. Gary really didn't expect to stay here, although he found that he liked the country better than he had expected. He had a teaching job back in Texas. It was a rural school and the school board had agreed to postpone the beginning of the term until the middle of October if he'd promise to be back by then. He and Dave would have the land by then or they'd never get it. October 4 was the deadline for them to appear together to claim it.

Gary wished he'd been raised to be a fighter instead of a teacher. He had never wanted or needed to be a fighter until now and his training as a teacher was worthless in this situation. If he could find Dave, he had no doubt that Dave could put Caleb Yount in his place in a hurry.

He slipped to the window and looked out. There was nothing there. There usually wasn't. Only Icky Minton used the alley regularly and Gary didn't want to see him. There was something about Icky that made him feel he could see through walls and hear a pin drop in a thunderstorm. Twice he had seen Yount out there. Because he knew Yount was looking for him, Gary kept hidden in the back room of the office.

Gary had never had to fight for what he wanted. Now that he was called on to fight, he didn't know how or have the stomach for it. He had never seen a man like Caleb Yount. For the first time in his life, he knew he had to fight to survive.

He wished he could talk to Mark Horn again. He had no idea what had happened to him. With Yount around, anything might have happened. When he first arrived in Monotony, Gary had seen the office with "Mark Horn, Attorney at Law" painted on the window, but the front door had been locked and people told him that Horn had moved to Omaha. Then only a couple of days later, he saw activity there, and he found the lawyer.

Horn had just arrived from Omaha. He hadn't expected Gary to get here from Texas so soon. Gary asked if he knew where his brother was, and Horn had said he had heard that he was here, too, out on Cottonwood Creek somewhere. He seemed nervous and in a hurry to get the brothers together so he could meet the conditions of the will, deliver their inheritance and go back to Omaha.

Gary had decided to ride up the Cottonwood and inquire about Dave until he found him. No one in town had seen Dave Paxton or, if he had, he wouldn't admit it.

Gary had gone to the livery barn to get his horse. That was when he first met Caleb Yount. Apparently not knowing Gary, Yount had found out which horse was his and had waited near that stall. Yount had invited Gary to go with him to the creek. But Gary had said he had other things to do. That's when Yount produced the gun like the strike of a snake. Yount shoved Gary out the back of the barn, leaving his horse there. Then he marched him across the corral which fenced in a short section of the creek so the horses always had running water in the corral. Climbing out of the corral, Yount directed Gary up the creek to the big bluffs just on the other side of the cottonwood grove.

There, Yount had demanded that Gary ride out of the country and not look back. When Gary said he had come to find his brother, Yount hit him. That seemed to trigger something in the big man, and he began beating Gary with a passion. Gary tried to defend himself, but he had no chance against the big man.

He was almost senseless when Yount stopped pounding on him. Yount stepped back, panting as if he'd run a mile, and glared at Gary.

"That's just a sample of what you'll get if you don't get out of this country," he said. "How about it? Are you going?"

Gary hadn't been able to think straight then. He didn't want Yount to begin beating him again, so he agreed to get out as soon as he was able.

"Make that immediately," Yount had growled. "I don't want to kill you. But if I catch you in town tomorrow at this time, I'm going to kill you or at least make you wish I had. Have I made myself clear?"

Gary had nodded, not trusting his voice to say anything. Yount had stepped back against the bluff, and Gary took that as a signal for him to go. He found he could barely stand, but he staggered down the creek toward town. He'd have to get his horse to get away.

Somewhere in the grove of cottonwoods that grew on both banks of the creek, he dropped down and stuck his face in the water. He felt better after he had splashed water over his head and gently rubbed the many bruised spots on his face and chest.

Yount hadn't given him any reason for the beating. He hadn't even identified himself. To Gary, he was just a kill-crazy bully. He seemed to go wild when Gary said he was here to look for his brother. Maybe the man was really crazy.

When Gary had recuperated some from his beating, he went on into town. It was dark then, and he went to the lawyer's office. It was closed. He saw a man on the street and asked if Mark Horn stayed at the hotel. He was told that Horn had a house back a block north of Norrid's big place. He'd had that before he moved to Omaha and hadn't sold it or his office when he moved.

Gary found Horn's house and was invited inside. Horn gasped in shock when he saw Gary and set about doctoring him as best he could. When he asked who had beaten him, Gary described the man. Before he had finished, Horn sat down, shaking his head.

"That's Caleb Yount," he said, his voice trembling. "I was hoping he'd never catch up with us."

"Who is Caleb Yount?"

"Joshua Greer's stepson. Joshua married Caleb's mother when Caleb was about fourteen. Joshua couldn't handle Caleb, and his mother wasn't much better so Joshua made the best of a bad bargain and pulled stakes between dusk and dawn. There was never a divorce so Caleb is claiming his rights as a son and is contesting the will that gives you and your brother this land."

"Can he do that?"

"Not if you and your brother meet the terms of the will and appear together before October 4. But if you fail, he just might make his claim stick."

"That's why he threatened to kill me if I didn't leave the country."

"Exactly," Horn said. "And he is just mean enough to do it too. If he can get rid of either you or Dave, then he might get the land. I don't think Joshua thought of that when he put that provision in his will."

"It should go to Dave," Gary said. "The only reason I'm named is so Dave and I will get together."

"That's right," Horn agreed. "But if you don't find Dave and appear in court together, Caleb Yount just might get that land. All he deserves is killing."

Gary did some hard thinking after he left the lawyer's house. In spite of his bruises, he resolved to stay and find Dave, if for no other reason than to keep Caleb Yount from getting that land.

Now as he considered things, he realized he could wait no longer to find his brother. He had thought when he holed up here in Horn's office that he could consult with the lawyer often, but Horn had never come back to his office.

Gary unbolted the door and stepped outside, then started down the alley. He'd have to watch for Yount. He hadn't seen him for more than a day, but he might still be around, waiting.

He'd have to have his horse, and it would be risky going into the barn to get him. As he passed behind the store, he saw the stranger who had been with Icky earlier. He was in the alley between buildings, but he was looking the other way into the street. Gary slipped past the narrow alley without drawing his attention.

From a rear corner of the pool hall, he saw a horse tied in front of the livery barn across the street. Maybe he could take that horse. Then he recognized the horse as his own. The livery barn owner must have rented him out to pay for the feed bill that Gary hadn't been around to pay. The horse was already saddled. Maybe his luck was changing.

Slipping down the alley between the feed store and the pool hall, he hit the street and crossed it. Just as he was untying the horse, he felt a jab in the small of his back.

"You don't take orders very well, do you?"

Gary's heart jammed into his throat, choking him. Yount had found him.

"Stealing horses ain't very smart in this country," Yount said softly. "Those cottonwood trees ain't worth much, but they sure can handle horse thieves."

Chapter 13

Dave Paxton was thoroughly frustrated, and frustration made him angry. He didn't doubt that Icky had thought he was directing him to Gary Wirth, but Paxton had found only a locked door at the lawyer's office.

Paxton had searched the town, not letting many people see him. He didn't know what Gary would look like, but he knew he'd be twenty-four, two years younger than he was. He hadn't seen Al Zamora since he left the pool hall. Zamora and Tug Buskey, the deputy, were the only two men in town that he felt he had to keep away from. He ducked into the store once, but Upshaw was still not there.

Just before leaving the alley between the store and the pool hall, he saw a stranger walking rapidly across the street from the feed store to the livery barn. Another man left the pool hall and ran toward him. Apparently they were friends. Probably worked together on a ranch somewhere, maybe the Circle N. He wanted nothing to do with any Circle N hands. He ducked back into the alley.

Maybe Icky could give him a new lead if he'd go back to see him. He'd need another pocketknife to give him. The only place to get that would be at the general store.

He was in the side street between the store and the bank then, so he turned toward the front of the store. Stepping out on the porch of the store, he glanced down at the front of the livery barn. The horse was still there but the men were gone. They had probably gone into the barn or back into the pool hall. His own horse was still tied to the hitchrack in front of the store.

Inside the store, he found a woman behind the counter but Upshaw was still missing. Paxton located the pocketknives and quickly picked out one and bought it. Icky would like it, maybe enough to make a special effort to find out where Gary Wirth was.

Paxton went outside again and turned toward the alley. He felt safer back there. Not so many people would see him. On the other hand, if someone wanted to kill him, he would be opening himself up to an ambush back here.

Reaching the back of the hotel, he

turned along the side and went down the steps to the door into Icky's little room. He knocked and waited until Icky peeked out. Slowly, almost reluctantly, Icky opened the door.

"I didn't find him, Icky," Paxton said. "Any other ideas where he might be?"

Icky shook his head. "He's been hiding in the back of that office, I think. It ain't locked. You could go right in."

"It was locked when I was there."

Icky frowned. "Then he is there and locked it from the inside. I ain't been down to see him. None of my business."

"I want you to make it your business," Paxton said. He pulled the new knife out of his pocket. "This is yours if you'll find out where Gary Wirth is. If you find him, tell him Dave Paxton will be in to see him."

Icky eyed the knife hungrily. "All right," he said finally, reaching for the knife. "If he's in town, I'll find him. And I'll tell him what you said."

"Good." Paxton went back through the door and up the steps.

At the top of the steps, he looked again at the lawyer's office. Icky had said that back door was unlocked. Crossing to the office, he tried the door. It opened to his touch. He stepped inside and looked at the door and the jamb beside it. He saw the bolt there. Someone had been in here, and he had bolted the door. Maybe this was Gary Wirth's hide-out. He wasn't here now, that was certain.

He stepped outside. Icky was just coming up the steps. It was probably time to do some of his chores, either at the hotel or the pool hall. He'd go back and ask Icky where Gary was likely to go.

Halfway to the hotel, he stopped suddenly as a man leaped around the back corner of the hotel. He barely had time to recognize Al Zamora before the gun in his hand spurted flame. The shot missed, and Paxton dug for his own gun.

Even at this distance, he could see the fear working in Zamora's face. He was too scared to hold his gun steady, but he was deadly dangerous, just the same. Paxton had his gun in his hand when Zamora fired his second shot. It missed too, and then Paxton's gun replied. Zamora was driven back against the corner of the hotel where he dropped his gun and clutched his arm.

Icky was screaming at Zamora. "You can't kill him! He's a ghost!"

Paxton didn't fire again. Zamora was disarmed. Even from here, Paxton could see that the wound was not a serious one, but it had stopped the Circle N gunman.

Icky was running to Zamora now that he saw that Paxton wasn't going to shoot again. Paxton started that way then stopped. He heard shouting back in the street and boots clumping on the board walk. Buskey was almost sure to be one of the men coming to see what had happened. If Paxton was here, Buskey would arrest him and throw him into jail again. Once was enough of that for Paxton.

Turning down the alley behind the buildings, he sprinted toward the other end of town. Dodging across the side street between the bank and the store, he ducked into the alleyway between the store and the pool hall. He heard yells and more running but most of it was up by the hotel now.

Racing to the street, he halted just short of the boardwalk and peeked out. There was no one close. His horse still stood at the hitchrack in front of the store.

Crossing the walk in two leaps, he reached the horse and jerked the reins loose. He mounted in one leap and nudged the old black horse into a gallop out of town.

He was almost past the livery barn when a shot echoed from back by the hotel. The range was too long for a six-gun but it told Paxton that he had been discovered. Glancing back, he saw no saddled horses on the street. It would take awhile for pursuit to organize, but it would come, he was sure.

Paxton pushed the old black horse as fast as he would go. He had asked a lot of the old horse the last day or two. He was too old to have to run like this. But Paxton's only chance was to put some distance between him and town before Buskey got a posse organized.

The old horse was well winded when Paxton came to the sod barn. Looking back, he could see the pursuit coming. They had gained on him, but they were too far behind to see that he had turned in at the barn.

He put the old black horse behind the hay and brought out the white one. Slipping on the long white coat and the big white hat, he led the horse outside. From there, he rode up the gully behind the barn and came out at the top of the bluff. Looking down, he saw Tug Buskey leading half a dozen men almost directly below him now.

Paxton took a deep breath and gave out his imitation of an Indian war cry. Dust flew as horses were skidded to a halt. Eyes whipped up to the top of the bluff. Paxton let them all get a good look at him before he pulled the horse back from the edge of the bluff. One wild shot came his way. When he nudged the horse out again to look down, he saw the entire posse spurring wildly back toward town, Tug Buskey in the lead. He gave another drawn-out whoop and the men below bent lower over their saddles and dug in their spurs viciously. The horses stretched out their strides as if they were in the greatest race of the century.

Paxton slowly rode his white horse back down the gully to the barn. That was one way to get a posse off his trail. Rooker had said that being a ghost would come in handy, but he hadn't figured it would be this convenient.

Paxton had barely gotten the white horse concealed behind the pile of hay in the barn and brought out the old black horse when he had company. Jeff Rooker came riding down the creek as if the entire Sioux tribe was just one jump behind him.

"Where's the Indians?" he demanded, sliding his horse to a halt. "I heard them howling."

Paxton laughed. "Ask Buskey and his posse, if you can catch them."

"Oh," Rooker said, light dawning in his face. "You're the palefaced, war-whooping Indian. Did Buskey see the ghost and run?"

"Fly would be a better word. He was trying to put wings on his horse."

"Wish I could have seen that," Rooker lamented. "Did you find any trace of your brother?"

"Icky showed me where he thought he was hiding, but I couldn't find him. He's in danger or he wouldn't be hiding. I've got to find him. I'd still be looking if Zamora hadn't thrown down on me and started shooting. I nicked him and took the fight out of him, but that brought Buskey and the whole town running. I was lucky to get away."

"Buskey may think twice before he chases you again," Rooker said with a grin. "He ain't any more ghost proof than Tidrow and his boys."

"I wish I could find that lawyer. He ought to know something about Gary. Since he lived here before he moved to Omaha, maybe he knows what happened to Joshua too."

"He was Joshua's friend," Rooker said. "I'll go to town and see if I can find any trace of him."

"I'll ride along," Paxton said. "If you find him, I want to talk to him."

He took off his white coat and hat, rubbed down the old black horse, then mounted. The horse was tired but Paxton hoped he wouldn't have to call on him to run again.

"We'll go by Sutcliffe's," Rooker said. "He hears a lot, being a preacher and visiting around quite a bit. He might know where Horn is."

Paxton didn't object, and they rode across the creek and up the road to Sutcliffe's. The preacher was home, his face long and haggard. His eyes suddenly bugged out as he looked at Paxton.

"I knew I'd seen that ghost before. It's you!" He backed away.

"You were too spooked last night to know what that ghost really looked like," Rooker said quickly. "From what I hear, it was the ghost of that killer, Kucek. Dave here does look like him. The town almost hanged him because everybody thought he was Kucek. But he ain't. I'll swear to that."

Sutcliffe stared at Paxton for another half minute then took a deep breath and turned back to Rooker. "I guess you wouldn't be riding with him if he was."

"That's a fact," Rooker said. "Have you seen Mark Horn lately?"

"I saw him once since he came back from Omaha," Sutcliffe said. "But he wasn't in church Sunday. Someone said he left town again. Maybe that ghost got him."

Rooker shot a glance at Paxton and grinned. "That ghost hasn't hurt anybody yet, has he?"

"I guess not," Sutcliffe admitted. "I've seen some strange things but nothing quite like that ghost on horseback."

Paxton and Rooker angled back toward the creek and the road to town. Rooker started chuckling before they were a quarter of a mile from Sutcliffe's.

"For a man who believes in the spirits coming back to talk to people, he sure don't take kindly to that ghost. Maybe it's all right for the spirits to talk to other people, but he wants no part in the conversation."

Paxton grinned. "He did shinny up that tree in fancy style when I came barging through Bertha's seance." His face sobered. "Maybe Horn went back to Omaha."

"It's possible," Rooker agreed. "I'll find out if anybody knows."

Paxton stopped in the grove just outside town while Rooker rode on into the main street. Monotony was no place for him this soon after Buskey had chased him out.

He watched for any activity around town while he waited. The livery barn was the nearest building to the grove, and he saw two horses, dried lather at withers and flanks, standing in front of the barn. Apparently, the men who had ridden them hadn't even bothered to rub the horses down. That irritated Paxton. A horse that had been run like that ought to have good care, at least.

The sun was still half an hour high when Rooker came back up the road, turning into the grove when he was even with Paxton.

"What did you find out?" Paxton asked, his impatience over the long wait coming to the surface.

"He ain't to be found. Upshaw said he had gone back to Omaha. Didn't know whether he'd come back to Monotony or not."

"I suppose that explains things."

Rooker shook his head. "I don't think so. Upshaw was saying words, but he was telling me something else."

Paxton frowned. "What do you mean by that?"

"Upshaw is half fat and all of it is yellow. Somebody told him to say that Horn is gone. I didn't believe a word he said."

"You think he's still here?"

"He's got a house just north of Norrid's. He may be a prisoner there. Even if you find your brother, you'll need a lawyer to handle the legal work to get your inheritance."

Paxton nodded. "Let's check and see."

"As soon as it's dark."

When darkness had settled over the town, Paxton and Rooker left the grove and circled above the town, reining up behind a little house north of Norrid's big one. Paxton couldn't see any light in the house, but they were still fifty yards from it. There might be a light in a window on the other side.

They left their horses and moved silently toward the house. Paxton felt like a pup stalking a twig. It was likely that there wasn't anyone in that house.

Rooker went to the left, Paxton to the right. Then, when Paxton was within ten feet of the house, a man leaped out at him. He made no sound but Paxton caught the gleam of a knife blade in the dim light. There was no mistaking his intentions.

Chapter 14

Paxton ducked and threw himself to one side. The big man swept low with the knife but missed. He wheeled, but by then, Paxton was on his feet again.

It was obvious that the man intended to kill him, but he evidently wanted to keep it quiet. Paxton wasn't in favor of attracting the attention of the town either.

The man came at Paxton again, still not touching the gun at his side. Paxton dodged away and jerked up his gun, but he didn't use it. When the man wheeled again, Paxton laid the barrel of the gun along the side of his head. He dropped the knife and slumped down in a heap.

Rooker came running around the house. "What's the ruckus?" he asked softly.

"Somebody wanted to draw and quarter me," Paxton said. "He must have something pretty valuable hidden in that house."

"Let's find out," Rooker said. Then he stooped over the man. "I've never seen him before. Have you?"

Paxton shook his head. "I'm not looking for friends like that."

Making sure the man was not moving, Paxton took his knife and his gun then followed Rooker to the door. It was unlocked and they pushed inside. It was too dark to see anything. Paxton struck a match while Rooker waited, gun in hand.

The big room they were in was empty, but the flare of the match brought a groan from the next room. Paxton stepped toward the partition door. His match went out and he had to strike another one. By its flickering light, he saw a man on the bed there.

"That's Horn," Rooker said. "Looks like he's more dead than kicking."

Paxton went to the bed. The match burned down to his fingers and he lit another one, looking around for a lamp. There was one on an old dresser and he lit it, putting the chimney back in place.

With lamp in hand, he returned to the bed. Rooker was already going over the injured man carefully.

"Beaten up like a steak ready for the skillet," Rooker said angrily. "Why would anyone do this to a man?"

"Can we get a doctor for him?"

"Ain't one closer than the county seat.

We'll have to do the best we can ourselves. Better check on that snake outside. If he's still there, maybe we ought to give him a sample of what he's given Horn."

Paxton stepped back outside. He didn't know how hard he had rapped that man but, after seeing the lawyer, he wanted to hit him a lot harder. But the man was gone. He had apparently come to, and found himself disarmed, so he ran. Paxton went back inside.

"He got away," he said. "We'll have to move Horn some place where he can't find him. Got any ideas?"

Rooker nodded. "If we put him over in the church, he wouldn't find him. I doubt if whoever did this is much of a church-goer. You watch him while I ride out and get Sutcliffe. It's his church."

Paxton nodded and did what little he could to make the lawyer easier. Then he blew out the light. That guard had been somebody who wanted the lawyer out of action. Since Horn was the one who was trying to bring Paxton and his brother together, it stood to reason that the man Gary Wirth was so afraid of was probably the one who had almost killed Mark Horn.

Paxton found a chair and sat just to one side of the window. If anybody came snooping around, he wanted to be the first to know it.

He heard nothing until Rooker came back with Sutcliffe. It was late; the town had gone to bed. Paxton waited in the doorway, his gun ready, until he was sure who his visitors were. Rooker had brought Sutcliffe up to date on the situation, and the preacher had agreed that the church was a good place to keep Horn until next Sunday. They'd have to move him before services.

Carefully, the three men lifted the wounded man in the blanket on which he was lying and carried him through the door. Having no wagon, they carried him down to the first bench above the creek on which the main part of town sat.

The church wasn't locked and Sutcliffe pushed the door open and Paxton and Rooker carried the lawyer inside. Sutcliffe cleared a spot in one of the front corners of the church.

"Make him as comfortable as you can," Sutcliffe said. "I'll go find Mrs. Fenton. She nurses every sick person in town. She's also a regular member of my congregation. I think she'll take care of Horn and not let anyone know he's here either."

"That's important," Paxton said. "Whoever beat him up like this will probably try to find him to keep him from telling who did it."

Paxton and Rooker arranged the extra blanket they had brought and laid Horn on it, covered by the one that had stayed on him as they carried him over.

"Not a very comfortable bed," Rooker said, "but it beats a coffin."

He went outside to stand guard beside the door until Sutcliffe brought the woman back to nurse the lawyer. Paxton sat beside Horn, wondering if he would ever recover.

Before Sutcliffe returned, Horn stirred uneasily and moaned. Paxton leaned over him. "Who did this, Mr. Horn?"

The lawyer's eyes came open slowly, and he tried to focus on Paxton's face. "Yount," he whispered. "Got to stay away from Yount."

Paxton wondered who Yount was, but he wouldn't waste the little energy Horn had by asking him to explain. He might have been the man Paxton had laid out with the gun barrel.

"Why did he do it?" he asked and leaned close for the answer.

"To keep brothers apart," Horn said.

"Dave Paxton and Gary Wirth?"

"Yes." The word was barely audible.

There was one more question Paxton wanted to ask. "Do you know who killed Joshua Greer?"

Horn didn't answer. Paxton leaned closer. He had passed out again. No telling when he would revive enough to answer more questions.

Sutcliffe came back with a big-boned woman who carried her age concealed behind a brusk facade of good health. Paxton would guess she wouldn't see sixty again, maybe not seventy.

"Mrs. Fenton is a good nurse," Sutcliffe said. "I've already told her how we found Mr. Horn. She understands the need for secrecy. You won't have to worry about them finding him unless they just stumble into the church."

"I'm guessing the only way they'll ever get inside a church is to be carried in," Rooker said. "I'm going home. Nothing we can do here that Mrs. Fenton can't do better."

After watching the woman fluff a couple of pillows she had brought and position them carefully around the wounded man, Paxton decided that Rooker was right. He went outside with Rooker, and they walked back to the place behind Horn's house where they had left their horses. They were still there.

As they started up the creek, Rooker asked, "Did he say anything?"

Paxton nodded in the dark. "He said Yount did that to him. Who is Yount?"

"Never heard of him," Rooker said.

"He must be the one that Gary is hiding from. If Horn is a sample of his work, I can see why Gary doesn't want to be caught."

"Seems to me like we'd better find out who Mr. Yount is and pay him a visit."

"Before he pays me a visit," Paxton added. "He seems to be intent on keeping Gary and me apart."

"Maybe he's the kind who does better fighting old men," Rooker said angrily. "Horn doesn't look like a fighter to me."

"My brother probably isn't either. His letters sound more like a schoolteacher, which is what he is."

"If we can find this bully, maybe we can give him a little schooling."

"It's my fight, not yours."

"I've taken a hand in your game," Rooker said, "partly because you're bellering at the same bull I am. This scrap with Yount has nothing to do with getting the man who killed Roy Greer, but if I can help, you can count on me."

It was good to have a friend like Rooker, Paxton thought, even if he did get him into some weird situations such as playing the ghost at Bertha's seance.

Paxton went on to Rooker's for the remainder of the night. He doubted if he would sleep much, worrying about Mark Horn and his brother. This unknown person, Yount, was going to have to be corralled and dehorned soon. The name Yount had a familiar ring to Paxton, but he could not remember where he'd heard it.

Paxton had considered the possibility that either he or his brother might be kept from appearing in time to claim that inheritance. But if Mark Horn should die from his beating, that would complicate things. Horn was Joshua's lawyer. Some other lawyer would take over the job of settling the estate but not in time to keep Gary and Paxton from losing the land. The deadline was only a few days away, and Horn's death wouldn't be likely to change that.

At breakfast, Paxton announced that he was going back to town to try to find Yount.

"You'll get yourself killed," Rooker said. "I'll go and you keep your pretty face out of sight. I'd like to find this Yount myself. And I'd like to know how Horn is doing."

Paxton didn't argue. Jeff Rooker could roam the town looking for Yount and checking on Horn with far less danger than Paxton could. But he'd make sure he was close enough to take up Yount's trail if Rooker uncovered it. When it came to a showdown with guns, Paxton would trust himself over Rooker, five to one.

Paxton waited in the grove while Rooker rode into town. It was almost noon when he came back, and Paxton was about ready to go look for him.

"Been hunting the town over for any sign of Yount. That man has the whole town buffaloed. You mention Yount and they clam up like they had glue in their mouths. Upshaw knows something about Yount just as sure as sunrise, but he ain't telling."

"What about Horn?"

"Still out of his head, but Mrs. Fenton says his fever is down. She thinks he'll pull through."

"We've got to find Yount before he finds Horn," Paxton said.

"Or you," Rooker added. "Or your brother. No dead bodies have turned up, so the odds are that your brother is still alive."

"After the way he beat up Horn, I wouldn't count on it," Paxton said.

"He sure ain't in town," Rooker said. "If

he is, he's hiding in some cellar. Horn can't tell us anything. Let's go see if we can learn anything about those holes around the spring. You did say there were some new ones there, didn't you?"

Paxton nodded. "I'm guessing there are. Norrid was mighty upset anyway. We're wasting time here, that's sure. If Horn doesn't come to and tell us something about Gary, I'll have to tear this town apart board by board till I find him."

They stopped at Rooker's place for a late dinner. Paxton told him the story of the train robbers burying their loot at a spring and that Joshua had thought this was the place. He didn't tell him that Joshua was one of the robbers.

"I've heard that story," Rooker said, eyes shining. "I've even seen the old holes somebody dug around the spring. But I thought that tale of buried gold was just a wild story. Maybe it's not. This might be our lucky day."

"If Joshua couldn't find the money, how can we expect to?"

"Luck," Rooker said, undaunted. "Think what a haul like that would mean."

"Could get our necks in a sling too," Paxton warned. "That's Circle N territory right now."

"We won't announce our arrival with bugles," Rooker said.

They got shovels and took a circular route to the spring. It was late afternoon when they pulled up behind a knoll shutting off the spring and the house from their view.

Paxton wasn't too excited about digging around the spring. He had to believe that Joshua had found the money if it was still there when he returned to the spring. He'd helped bury it; surely he'd known about where it was.

"I'm trying to think like an outlaw," Rooker said excitedly. "If I had to bury some money in a hurry at night, where would I put it?"

They dismounted and moved to the top of the knoll. There was no one at the spring, and even the house looked deserted. The sun was almost down. Paxton pointed to a big rock cropping out of the ground not far from the spring.

"Doesn't look like anybody has dug there," he said.

"Too far from the spring," Rooker said.

"But it's about the only landmark close to the spring."

"You're right," Rooker said excitedly. "Let's start there."

As twilight deepened and it became obvious there was no one around, not even at the house, they moved over the knoll, leading their horses. Close to the rock, they began digging, probing back under the rock. There was no evidence of digging here, but there were holes everywhere near the spring itself.

Darkness was settling down when Paxton heard running horses. He spoke softly to Rooker who jerked up his head. Paxton wheeled to stare into the gloom toward the Circle N, the direction from which the horses were coming. He saw them then, four riders. He and Rooker were caught like rats in a trap.

Chapter 15

Elias Norrid had a feeling there would be somebody digging at the spring. Now that he was proven right, it gave him another odd feeling. Was he getting to be like Bertha? Could he tell ahead of time what was going to happen?

It sent a shiver up his spine just thinking about it, but there was no denying the fact. He had known before they came in sight of the spring that there would be someone digging there. He hadn't even been surprised when he saw them. Still, it frightened him.

He jerked his thoughts back to the immediate business. He didn't have to consult his feelings to know what was going to happen to those two digging at the spring now. They were trespassing, and they would be shot.

"Kill them!" Norrid roared as the two men started running toward their horses. He turned his head toward Tidrow, riding beside him. "Who are they?"

"That one looks like Jeff Rooker," Tidrow said. "The other one looks like Kucek. Or his ghost."

"That ain't no ghost!" Norrid screamed.

He hated that word ghost. He'd had it flung at him so many times, and every time he heard it, he thought of that white rider coming at him on the pure white horse. Bertha insisted he had come in response to her calling, and nothing Norrid could say would change her mind. He wasn't so sure himself any more.

Ghost or no ghost, those two were digging for the money buried at the spring. If there was any money there, it was going to be his. He'd kill anyone who tried to take it from him.

"Sam," he yelled, "you and Vic get that so-called ghost. I'll take care of Rooker. But get him, no matter what you have to do."

Norrid didn't trust himself to shoot the ghost. Just thinking about the other night brought visions into his mind that blurred his shooting eye. Sam Tidrow and Vic Ortis were both excellent marksmen. If those two couldn't bring that ghost down, nobody could.

The two men had reached their horses now, but they were within range of the six-guns Norrid and his men had. Norrid opened up the firing by aiming at Rooker. He missed. Rooker swung into the saddle and kicked his horse into a run.

"Shoot! Shoot!" Norrid screamed at the other two men. What were they waiting for? Did they want to see if that one would turn into a white ghost on a white horse?

Tidrow and Ortis began firing, both aiming at the rider who had angled a few feet away from Rooker. Although both of them emptied their guns, the rider didn't even flinch. Complete misses. Norrid couldn't believe his eyes.

The riders hadn't fired a shot in return, and now they charged up the slope behind the spring and into the choppy hills. They were disappearing from sight. Tidrow and Ortis stopped to reload their revolvers. Norrid yanked up his horse too. Loanda reined up with them. She seemed to be going along just for the fun of it.

"How could you both miss with every shot?" Norrid yelled. "He was as plain as the sky at sunrise!"

Tidrow shook his head. "I thought I had him in my sights. Maybe he is a ghost."

"Don't say that!" Norrid roared. "A ghost would just sail off into the sky."

"Why should he?" Ortis asked. "If we

can't hit him, he might as well stay here and laugh at us."

Norrid wheeled on Loanda. "Why weren't you shooting?"

Loanda shrugged. "Why should I waste bullets? Nobody is going to hit a ghost." She chuckled. "Anyway, I don't like ghost meat."

Norrid felt sick. Loanda was making fun of them all. There wasn't such a thing as a ghost. Bertha couldn't make him believe it. Neither could Sam Tidrow or Loanda. But deep inside, he had a shaky feeling as if he were standing on quicksand. How much more proof was it going to take to make him believe? No man could ride that close in front of two expert shots like Sam Tidrow and Vic Ortis and let them empty their guns at him and not be killed. That rider hadn't even flinched. He simply hadn't been hit. Unless . . . those bullets went right through him like they would through smoke. If he was really a ghost . . . Norrid shook his head. It was getting to him, but he'd never let them see it.

He must be catching it from Bertha. She was so sure that she could bring spirits to earth, she had laid claim to bringing that ghost to her seance the other night. She really believed it. She had told everybody who would listen that the ghost's message was "Death to the killers." Norrid had heard those words himself, but he wouldn't have thought of them again if Bertha hadn't reminded him over and over.

Bertha said it had to be the ghost of the man burned in that homesteader's house. The killers would be the ones who had set the fire. Norrid was one of those. So was Tidrow and Ortis and Zamora. They weren't all going to die. In fact, none of them was going to die!

He glanced at Tidrow and Ortis as they finished loading their guns. Was he imagining it or were their hands shaking? Did they really believe that they'd been shooting at a ghost? They couldn't hit the side of a barn with hands shaking like that. He glanced at Loanda. She was as calm as an old lady at a Sunday School picnic.

"You're sure taking it easy," he snorted.

"Why not?" she asked with a shrug. "Ghosts don't hurt anybody."

"This one does," Ortis snapped. "He shot Zamora."

"He's not hurt bad," she said.

"He'll be back at work in a day or two," Tidrow agreed. "It could have been worse. Al said he had this jasper dead center in his sights, and he missed."

"You can cheer him up by telling him he's not the only one," Loanda said easily.

"We've got to stop these outsiders from digging at this spring," Norrid snapped.

"Maybe you ought to set up a guard day and night," Ortis suggested.

"Not a bad idea," Norrid agreed. "Those guards will shoot on sight anybody who starts to dig anywhere on this property."

"Want to see what those two were doing?" Tidrow asked.

"Looked to me like they had just started," Norrid said. "You can look. I have to get home. Bertha, in spite of all her spooky seances, is afraid to be alone at night."

Norrid turned his horse down the creek. Loanda added more uneasiness to his thoughts by calling after him that the ghost had gone this way. He might run into him.

Norrid almost yanked his horse around. But that would have been an admission that he was afraid. He wouldn't allow anyone to know that. Rooker and that ghost had come this way. He'd have to go almost seven miles down the creek, and the ghost could jump out at him at any time.

He remembered Loanda saying that ghosts don't hurt people. Maybe it would scare him, but if it didn't hurt him, he'd make out. Then he remembered that Ortis said that the ghost had wounded Al Zamora. The cold knot in his stomach was so big he was almost sick.

As he rode, he thought of what had led up to this. Maybe it was Bertha and her seances. He wished his sister had some other hobby. Perhaps it had been a mistake taking Bertha in to keep house for him after his wife died. He had thought that was a wonderful idea at the time. But then came these seances. Bertha wasn't interested in the money at the spring. If she'd use her power to talk to the spirits to find out exactly where that money was, he would believe in her seances. So far, her seances had only brought trouble.

He had never had any faith in spirits. But after what had happened the last few days, he was beginning to think he was wrong. Maybe he should believe. Perhaps if he did, the ghosts would let him alone. Bertha said that spirits would haunt anyone who refused to believe in them.

There could be no doubt about that ghost at the seance. He'd had a close look at him, entirely too close a look. And tonight two men had fired ten shots at the same man, or ghost, and missed every one. There had to be some kind of explanation that ordinary reasoning couldn't provide. One thing was sure, if that ghost could be killed, it had to be done.

With so many people suddenly digging at the spring, Norrid had to believe that there really was money buried there. Surely so many people couldn't all be wrong. He wished his lawyer would hurry up with the legal details so he could own that spring. He said that it was still tied up in Joshua Greer's estate. He'd tie that lawyer up in some kind of knot if he didn't get a clear title to that land soon.

Loanda was keeping other squatters off the land for now. Technically, she was a squatter herself. If the Greer heirs showed up, they'd have to be eliminated. Roy Greer had been taken care of. Norrid's lawyer had said that Dave Paxton, raised by the Greers, might inherit the spring. Joshua Greer hadn't lived on the land long, but he had taken a preemption, not a homestead. He had paid out in a year and had owned the land clear when he died.

It could have been Paxton that they had killed in that fire. If so, Paxton looked a lot like Kucek. Norrid wasn't sure. Somehow that man hadn't really looked like Kucek. His features were similar, but Kucek was a hard man, a killer. This man wasn't.

Norrid hoped it had been Paxton who had died in that fire.

His horse suddenly pricked up its ears, and Norrid twisted to stare into the dark beside the trail. At that instant, a squall, something between an Indian war whoop and a lion's roar, erupted not ten feet from him. Fear exploded inside Norrid, and he screamed and dug in his heels, sending his horse at breakneck speed down the road.

He didn't slow down until he hit town. Putting his horse in the barn, he stripped the saddle off him, then stepped outside and came face to face with the ghost again. His heart seemed to stop beating for a moment then began going double time. But was this the ghost? This was Felix Kucek, no doubt about that, but was it the same man he'd seen riding that white horse?

"Been waiting for you to get home," Kucek growled. "You run around worse than a young buck chasing the girls."

"Been out to my ranch," Norrid managed to say. "What do you want?"

"I want back on the payroll," Kucek said. "Two hundred a month."

"Two hundred?" Norrid exploded, his choking fear suddenly jarred out of him. "You ain't worth ten unless you're killing somebody."

"Two hundred," Kucek repeated calmly. "Or I spread the word that you hired the two Greers killed."

"If you told anybody that, they'd hang you for murder."

"Think so? It wouldn't be me they'd go after. It would be you. By the time they finished with you, I'd be gone."

Norrid knew Kucek was right. They'd be afraid to tackle Kucek. But there were some in Monotony who would delight in hanging Norrid for murder. Kucek held the high cards, and he knew it. Norrid knew it too.

"All right," he said finally. "But if you get paid two hundred a month, you'll have to do some jobs for me."

"I didn't say I'd balk at doing my kind of work. I've always lived by what my gun earned for me. I figure that ain't going to change."

Norrid resolved in his mind to get rid of Kucek at the first opportunity. That decision came as quickly as had the one to knuckle under and pay Kucek what he demanded. Maybe he'd give the job of eliminating Kucek to Ortis. He claimed to be tough and a master with a gun. Even Ortis would have to ambush Kucek though. Norrid didn't care how he did it just so it was done.

As long as Kucek was alive and back on his payroll, he might as well be given a job to earn his money.

"Ride out to the Circle N," Norrid said. "Tell Tidrow that I've hired you again. As long as you're working for me, you can kill a man for me. I don't know his name. They all call him the ghost, but he's no ghost. You can get him."

"Sure thing," Kucek said. "I make ghosts, but I don't believe in them coming back."

Norrid watched Kucek get his horse from the side of the barn and ride slowly out of town and up the creek. He turned to the house. Maybe Bertha could tell him what to expect now. He was at his wit's end.

Bertha was amazed when he asked her to give him a prediction on who along the Cottonwood would die next.

"I thought you didn't believe in my predictions," she said.

"Just tell me what you see," Norrid snapped.

"Leave me alone so I can consult the spirits."

He went into his bedroom, glad to get away from the mumbling that Bertha did when she was supposed to be talking to the spirits.

When he came out of his room after her incantations had stopped, he demanded, "Well, what did you find out?"

"I saw the spirit returning," she droned. "He will tell you what you must do."

Norrid frowned. That was no answer, but it promised one. He didn't believe, he told himself again. But after all that had happened, he was afraid not to believe.

Chapter 16

Paxton heard the snap of the bullets past him, and one nicked his hat, twisting it on his head. He didn't even bother to straighten it. This was no time to stand and fight, either. The odds were against him.

Ducking low over his horse, he kicked the old black into as fast a run as the horse could muster. Each second, he expected to feel the burn of a bullet or to have the old black stumble and fall. Neither happened, and then the shooting stopped as suddenly as it had begun.

Looking back, he saw that the men had halted their horses and appeared to be reloading their guns. Relief swept over him. By the time they had their guns reloaded, he and Rooker would be out of range. Neither had fired a shot in return. The situation was not right for a battle.

They went over the knoll and wheeled their horses down the valley. Once beyond sight and sound of the spring, Paxton turned to Rooker.

"Are you all right?"

"Sure," Rooker said. "How about you? I think they were shooting at you more than me."

"Maybe they recognized me as their ghost," Paxton said with a grin. "They missed."

"I don't know how," Rooker said. "They were practically on our backs."

"If they thought I was a ghost, they might have been too nervous to hold their guns steady."

Rooker reined in his horse to keep pace with the rapidly slowing old black horse. "That has to be it. I told you it was wise to be a ghost."

"I'd rather be a ghost they didn't shoot at," Paxton said.

"Doesn't look like they're going to come after us," Rooker said, hipping around in the saddle.

"Maybe they just wanted us off the spring. They must think there is something there too. If they're not going to chase the tails off us, I think I'll look some more for Gary."

"You'd better be careful. You're not a cat with nine lives. You can't always be as lucky as you were back there, ghost or no ghost."

"I think I might have better luck at night when nobody can see me. Can you think of anyplace outside town where Gary might be hiding out?"

Rooker nodded slowly. "There should be better places to hide outside town than inside because nobody is liable to look beyond the town limits. Have you thought about the caves in the bluffs along the creek?"

"Not for a hideout for Gary," Paxton admitted. "I have seen the caves and wondered how deep they are and if a man could hide in there."

"Some of them aren't much more than a hole under a cliff, but some are deep enough for a man to set up housekeeping inside. Maybe you ought to check out some of the biggest ones."

"This man, Yount, might be living in one," Paxton said.

"Maybe," Rooker agreed. "If you decide to explore any of them, you don't want to barge in like a bear after honey. You could get stung real good if you found his hideout."

"Can I find those caves at night?" Paxton asked.

"Sure. Especially if you wait till the moon comes up. You'll find the caves in the chalk bluffs just under those rock rims."

"I'll take a look," Paxton said. "I'll let you know what I find."

He nudged the old black on down the valley while Rooker reined off toward his dugout. With his eyes scanning the bluff on his left, he watched for any dark spot that might be a cave. The first place where the chalk rocks jutted out didn't seem to have any caves. He had just reached the second area where the bluffs showed a promise of caves when he heard a horse behind him.

Reining off the trail into the rocks along the base of the bluff, he dismounted. With one hand close to the black's nose to cut off any nicker and with his other hand on his gun, he waited.

A rider materialized on the road, scanning the bluffs and the creek as if expecting something to jump out at him. Paxton recognized Elias Norrid. Even in the deep shadows, Paxton could sense the fear that rode with the banker.

As Norrid passed the place where Paxton was hiding close to the road, his horse pricked up its ears and threw its head toward them. Norrid heaved himself around in the saddle to stare into the darkness.

Paxton reacted instantly. If he didn't, he knew the banker might decide to shoot in his direction. He gave a wild whoop that startled even his old black. Norrid's horse snorted in fear and sidestepped. As soon as Norrid could right himself in the saddle, he squalled at the horse like a cat with its tail caught in the door and drummed his heels against the horse's sides. The horse hit the road in a wild run, thundering toward town like the devil was clutching his tail.

Paxton couldn't help laughing. Bertha's seances and Norrid's experience the other night in the grove had made a shambles of the banker's nerves. Paxton doubted if he would let the horse slow down until he hit town.

He turned his attention back to the dark spots under the cliffs. There he found two caves. But when he ground reined the old black and tried to go into the caves, he found them to be very shallow. A few feet from the opening of each, the floor rose and the ceiling lowered until he could go no farther. No one could live in either of those caves.

Mounting, he rode on down the creek, exploring each cave he found. The fourth one he came to was much deeper than the others with a roof that allowed him to stand upright several feet back from the mouth. He struck a match and moved back into the cave. There was no sign that anyone had ever tried to live here.

He was too far from town, he decided. If Gary was holed up in a cave, it likely would be one much closer to town where he surely expected to meet Paxton and the lawyer, Horn.

Still, as he moved down the valley, he didn't want to pass up any caves. The very one he passed up might be the one Gary would be hiding in. Although he explored a dozen caves along the left side of the creek, he found no one in any one of them. Finally, near town, he gave up in disgust and turned his horse into the road. He had looked in most, if not all, of the caves along the creek.

He decided it must be nearly midnight. If Horn was able to talk, he could talk as well at midnight as any other time. Maybe the lawyer could give him some ideas as to where Gary might be.

He had kept an eye out for Elias Norrid. The banker had been moving mighty fast after Paxton had yelled at him back there. But he could have stopped for some reason and Paxton certainly didn't want to overtake him.

There were only a few lights anywhere in town when Paxton reached the cotton-wood grove. He rode carefully through the grove and kept close to the creek until he was almost past town. The church was on the end of the main street on the side nearest the creek at the lower end of town.

Tying his horse to a tree that was well below the main grove, he moved silently up the bank to the first bench of land above the creek. The church loomed up ahead of him. There might be a side or back door, but Paxton hadn't discovered it. He really hadn't paid much attention to the church except when they had moved Mark Horn into it. They had carried him in the front door.

Stopping at the side of the church near the front, he studied the main street. There were no lights there now. The only lights in town showed in a couple of windows in houses back from the main street.

Moving around the corner, Paxton pushed the church door open and stepped quickly inside. He heard a low gasp and decided that must be Mrs. Fenton. What would she do? Would she shoot?

"It's me, Dave Paxton," he said softly. "Is Mr. Horn awake?"

There was no answer for a long time.

Paxton began to feel prickles running up his neck. Maybe some one had found the lawyer and was just waiting for those who had hidden him here to come back so they could get them too. Then a small voice answered faintly.

"He's much better. He may be awake."

Paxton moved softly forward to the corner where they had put Mark Horn. Mrs. Fenton had spoken from the opposite corner. The darkness was thick enough to cut inside the church.

"Mr. Horn?" Paxton said, stopping near the corner.

"Who are you?" The voice was weak but demanding.

"Dave Paxton. Do you feel like talking?"

"Don't let him get too tired," Mrs. Fenton warned. "I'm going out to walk around while you're here to watch him."

She moved silently out the front door and Paxton turned back to the lawyer. "Do you know where Gary Wirth is?"

"No," Horn said. "But you must find him quickly. His life is in danger. So is yours."

"I can take care of myself. Where do you think I might find my brother?"

"I wish I knew. Yount tried to make me tell him where he was or where you were. I told him I didn't know, but he didn't believe me."

"Who is Yount?"

"Caleb Yount. He's as mean as ugly sin. I'm sure Gary is still around. I talked to him twice. Be careful. Yount will ambush you if he gets a chance. He's afraid of your reputation. Yount will inherit that land if you brothers don't. I think he'll kill to keep you from getting it." Horn had talked rapidly, and now he seemed to collapse from the effort.

"Who is Yount?" Paxton repeated, but Horn didn't answer.

Paxton leaned over Horn. He had passed out. Paxton went outside where he met Mrs. Fenton returning to her vigil. He didn't know where to start looking now for Gary, but he felt he couldn't wait until morning to resume the search. Mark Horn had sounded urgent. Besides, he might have better luck staying alive himself at night. Since he hadn't found Gary in the caves he explored, maybe he was in town.

He thought of Horn's warning about Caleb Yount. That name still haunted him. Suddenly he remembered where he had heard it. Yount was the name of the widow Joshua Greer had married. She'd had a big bully of a son. Between the son and his mother, Joshua soon had more than he could take of domestic life and he left. This Yount that Horn had talked about, the one who had beaten him almost to death, must be that widow's son. He apparently thought he could inherit the land that Joshua had owned if he could keep the two brothers named in Joshua's will from meeting the terms of that will. He probably had a good chance of succeeding, Paxton admitted.

Paxton went up to the next bench of land above the level where the business section of town stood. He checked the two homes here that still had lights. He didn't recognize anyone in the one house. The other house was Norrid's, and the whiteheaded banker was pacing the floor in the big room, obviously worried.

Paxton moved on. After going past Horn's little house, he turned back to the business section of town, realizing how impossible his search was. As he passed the hotel, he thought of checking the register, but he knew Gary wouldn't risk staying there. As he started to step off the porch on the walk toward Horn's office, a gun roared and splinters from the corner of the hotel slapped him in the face.

Horn's warning that Yount would try to ambush him rang through his mind.

191

Chapter 17

Gary Wirth heard the shot over by the hotel. He hadn't really been asleep. He never really slept any more. He was always half awake, tense, ready to leap for his life at a second's notice. That shot had sounded like that notice.

Moving quickly to the tiny knothole he'd discovered in the back room of Mark Horn's office when he'd first found this place to hide, he pressed an eye to it and looked out. The office was between the bank and the hotel and so near the very center of Monotony's activity that there was little danger of being found as long as he kept quiet.

The moon was up now, and it illuminated the near side of the hotel. Gary saw a man sprawled on the porch near the corner. His first thought was that he was dead. Then he saw that he had thrown himself back there. Apparently, he had been shot at as he stepped off the end of the porch.

His eye flashed to the back of the hotel. He saw a heavyset man at that corner, a gun in his hand. Caleb Yount! Gary would know that squat figure anywhere.

Dropping back, he considered the situation. The man at the front of the hotel would surely duck back inside. He probably wasn't even sure where the bullet had come from. Maybe he'd been hit. Gary couldn't be sure.

He had no idea who he was. But if Yount was trying to kill him, that automatically made him Gary's ally. Pressing his eye to the hole again, he saw the man on the porch inching toward the corner. When he showed himself this time, Yount might be lucky and get him. The man probably thought that the ambusher had left after failing with his first shot, but Yount was waiting expectantly.

Reaching back in his bunk against the wall, Gary grabbed his gun. It was dark in the back room, but he knew every inch of it by heart.

Slipping to the doorway, he inched his way outside. The moon didn't hit the back side of the office, and he was in shadow when he stepped outside. From here, he could have shot at Yount. But it would give away his hiding place, and his life depended on that remaining a secret. It had saved him twice now.

Gliding around the corner, he ran between the office and the bank to the front of the bank, across the porch, and then back the length of the building to the rear. Every rock he stepped on reminded him that he had forgotten to pull on his boots. From here, he could see the back corner of the hotel and Caleb Yount. Yount was still waiting like a cat poised at a mouse hole. Gary couldn't see the front of the hotel where the other man was.

He saw Yount bring the gun up. Apparently, he had heard or seen something that told him the man was about to show himself. Gary cocked his gun and waited. He wouldn't shoot if he didn't have to. A shot would draw attention to him and he didn't want that unless it was unavoidable.

He saw Yount suddenly lift his gun to eye level. Gary already had his gun up and cocked. He pulled the trigger. He knew he hadn't hit Yount. He wasn't sure he'd even tried to hit him. It wasn't in him to kill a man. Yount dived back around the corner of the hotel. Gary expected him to turn his gun on him. But in a couple of seconds, he saw him dashing away from the back of the hotel toward the houses up on the second bench above the creek.

He could have gotten a good shot at him now, but he had done all he had intended to do. He had kept him from killing the man at the front of the hotel. Turning, he glided back along the side of the bank and across the porch at the front. The moonlight didn't hit him here, and he felt a little safer. But he didn't feel completely safe until he had reached the rear of the lawyer's office and gone through the back door.

He wished he knew who the man on the hotel porch was. Pressing his eye to the knothole, he saw that he was gone. That was good. He didn't want anyone to fall into the clutches of Caleb Yount, no matter who he was.

The last time he'd seen Yount, except at a safe distance, was the day he'd tried to take his own horse from the front of the livery barn. Yount had jabbed a gun in his ribs and accused him of horse stealing. If it hadn't been so dark that no one could see him, he was sure that Yount would have killed him. But the livery man came out before Yount could take him anywhere and asked what he was doing.

Gary hadn't liked the livery man very much but he had looked like an angel to him then. Gary had quickly stated that he'd seen his horse here and was taking him into the barn. The livery barn owner agreed that it was Gary's horse. Yount could do nothing but back off. Gary had gone into the barn and stayed until he got the chance to slip away without Yount seeing him.

Gary wished he'd been able to zero in on Yount just now when he'd had the chance. If he could have killed him or at least wounded him severely, it would have made life livable again for him. He had only a few more days to find his brother and claim that land, and about all he had done was hide. He was going to have to take some risks.

He had slipped unnoticed into the pool hall one evening and listened to the talk. Everybody seemed to be talking about the ghost of a gunfighter on a white horse. Gary didn't believe in ghosts, but because Dave Paxton was a gunfighter and Mark Horn had said he thought he was around Monotony somewhere, Gary thought this "ghost" could be his brother.

Gary was awake before dawn, as usual. He ate some of the canned things he had slipped out of Upshaw's store one night when he had run out of supplies. He hadn't had anything hot to eat for so long that he thought his stomach would cry "Fire" if anything warm came down.

Slipping out of his little room, he moved between the bank and the office to the street. Maybe he could get a horse now before the town woke up. He saw that some of the town was already awake. A woman was coming across the street from the church, of all places. She was headed directly for the alley between Horn's office and the bank. He pressed himself back against the wall and waited. When the woman stepped into the alley, he spoke softly.

"Don't be scared, ma'am. Who did you see over in the church?"

The woman gasped but held her ground. She stared at Gary a minute before she spoke. "I can't tell you anything," she said finally. "Who are you?"

"I'm looking for Mark Horn," Gary said. "Do you know where he is?"

She stared at him again then brushed past him. "I have to get something."

He watched her go around the corner, and he was sure she went into the back door of the office where he'd been sleeping. It would be too dark in there for her to see his bunk, but it suddenly hit him that if she had to get something from

Horn's office, it must be for the lawyer. Was the lawyer hiding in the church?

Checking the empty street, Gary hurried across to the church and went inside. His eyes quickly adjusted to the darkness inside, and he moved down the aisle. Then he heard something in the corner. Moving closer, he saw the man on the bed of quilts.

"Mr. Horn!" Gary exclaimed, dropping beside him. "What happened?"

Horn looked at Gary. "Never mind me. Find your brother. He was here last night looking for you."

"I want to find him," Gary said. "But where is he?"

"I imagine he's out on the Cottonwood, maybe at the dugout where they tell me Jeff Rooker lives."

"Are you going to be all right?" Gary asked.

"With Mrs. Fenton taking care of me, I should. Just so long as Yount doesn't find me."

Gary nodded. "I'll find Dave if I can and bring him back. He'll take care of Yount."

Running to the door, he looked up and down the street. It was still empty. He hurried across the street to the alley where he met Mrs. Fenton again. She brushed past him and hurried toward the church. Gary slipped into the back room of the office and waited for the town to come alive. He had to have more ammunition for his gun. Upshaw's was the only place he could get it.

When his watch told him Upshaw would be open, he slipped outside and down the back alley behind the bank to the rear of Upshaw's store. From there he moved around to the front and walked in the door. Upshaw was alone in the store, sweeping the floor in preparation for the day's business.

Upshaw observed Gary with a critical eye as he picked out a box of ammunition and paid for it.

"How far to Jeff Rooker's place?" he asked.

"What difference does that make?" Upshaw demanded.

"I'm a friend of his. I want to visit him."

Upshaw clearly doubted that, but he finally told Gary it was six miles, then described the dugout where Rooker lived.

"Is he looking for you?" Upshaw asked.

Gary frowned as he watched the pig-eyed merchant. He hadn't wanted to wait on Gary. Had someone like Yount warned him not to sell anything to him? Would

Upshaw run to Yount with the news that Gary was riding up the creek to Rooker's this morning?

"It will be a surprise," Gary said and hurried out of the store. His only hope would be to get his horse and get out of town before Yount was around to watch for him.

He crossed the empty street and went behind the blacksmith shop. The livery barn was half a block up from the blacksmith shop, but he didn't want to risk going in the front door of the barn.

He had just started to step out from behind the blacksmith shop when he saw Yount appear at the corner of the livery barn, almost as if he were watching for Gary to show up to get a horse. Likely that was his usual station every morning, making sure that Gary didn't try to get out of town.

Gary stepped back. Yount hadn't seen him, but if he was in the street now, Gary couldn't even get back across the street to the lawyer's office. He took a deep breath. He'd spent almost all his time hiding since he'd come to Monotony. He couldn't beat Yount by hiding. He had to find his brother.

If he couldn't get a horse here in town,

maybe he could get one some place up the valley. Using the blacksmith shop to block out the front of the livery barn, he slipped down to the creek. There he turned upstream, small trees and the creek bank hiding his movements.

When he got to the grove, he thought he had finally escaped from Yount. It would be a long walk, but somewhere he'd get a horse.

He was beyond the grove at a place where the chalk bluffs rose above the right bank of the creek when he thought he heard a horse above him on the bluffs. He ducked into a depression and watched. His heart sank when he saw Yount riding along the rim of the bluff, looking down. Upshaw must have told Yount about Gary's question.

He waited there until Yount came back, and then he slipped out and hurried on up the creek. He tried to keep a sharp eye on the bluffs and his back trail. He didn't see anything, and he was beginning to think he had given Yount the slip.

He was passing a little gully that had been washed in the face of the bluff by rain when he felt something slap his shoulders. Before he could reach up, his arms were pinned to his side. A delighted laugh came from the gully, and Yount stepped out, holding the rope tight. Despair and fear washed over Gary.

"Figured you'd be along," Yount said, taking Gary's gun. "Looking for your brother, I reckon. I'll take you to a place you haven't looked yet. Come on."

Gary was almost dragged off his feet as Yount started back down the valley, pulling Gary as fast as he could walk. Gary tried to hold back but was yanked along with an ease that told him he wasn't strong enough to resist.

Less than a quarter of a mile from the spot where he'd been roped, Gary was dragged into a cave that showed signs of habitation. This apparently was the place where Yount had stayed when he hadn't been in town watching for Gary.

There was a big rock back in the cave that had a natural crease around the middle. Yount pushed Gary down beside the rock and wrapped the rope around the rock, fitting it into that crease.

"Now I figure you'll stay put for a while," he said. "I just want to keep you safe where you won't find your brother. A few more days, and it won't make any difference."

Gary knew that was a lie. Yount

wouldn't dare let Gary live. If Gary could prove what Yount had done to him, Yount would lose the inheritance and maybe his freedom as well.

"I'll take good care of you," Yount said, "providing you tell me where your brother is. I'd rather have him than you."

"I don't know where he is," Gary said. "Why should I tell you anyway?"

"Because if you know something and won't tell me, you'll look worse than that lawyer does."

"If I knew where he was, I'd have found him," Gary said.

"That means you think he is up the creek. I'll look."

Yount left the cave, and Gary tried desperately to get out of the ropes. But five minutes of hard struggle proved that he couldn't get loose. He'd be here until Yount decided to turn him loose. And that would never happen, he was sure.

Chapter 18

Dave Paxton knew he'd been mighty lucky to escape that ambush at the hotel. That first shot should have nailed him. He was sure the man was near the rear of the hotel, and he had been ready to dive out and take his chances on a showdown when someone behind the bank had taken a hand. That one shot had apparently ended the fight.

Paxton had run back around the other side of the hotel, thinking he might get a shot at the ambusher, but there was nobody there when he arrived. He knew he had to get out of town. Those shots would surely bring someone to investigate. It would likely be Tug Buskey, the deputy.

Hurrying to his horse at the creek behind the church, he mounted and headed upstream. He was frustrated at not finding his brother, but he'd take up the search again tomorrow.

He spent the night at the sod barn and went on up to Jeff Rooker's the next morning. Rooker seemed particularly glad to see him.

"Wondered if you'd run into trouble," Rooker said. "What did you find in the caves?"

"A lot of dirt and rocks," Paxton said. "Nobody in any of them. I did get ambushed at the hotel in town, but the bushwhacker missed."

"There's a man here now who won't miss if he tries it," Rooker said.

"Somebody I haven't already met?"

"If you'd met him, you'd probably be dead," Rooker said solemnly. "Awhile after I got home last night, I heard a rider coming. I thought it was you, so I went outside to ask what you'd found. Then before I got out where he could see me, I noticed his horse wasn't black: it was gray. I took a good look at the rider. It was Kucek, the man who shot Roy Greer. I ran back for my gun, but he was gone by the time I got it. He was heading for the Circle N, I think."

"He'll probably be looking for me," Paxton said.

"Sure as sunrise. Norrid has hired him before."

"If he's the man who killed Roy, he's the man I want," Paxton said. "He may have killed Joshua too."

"Don't let him get the drop on you," Rooker warned. "He's a cold-blooded killer."

"I want him as bad as he could possibly want me," Paxton said. "Since Gary wasn't holed up in one of the caves, do you have any idea where he might be?"

"Town's the best bet," Rooker said. "There just ain't many other places for him to hide. But you'd better stay out of town in daylight. If you've got to look, do it after dark."

"Will Kucek go into town?"

"Might," Rooker said. "He stayed at the hotel before. I figure he spent last night at the Circle N. He may stay there till his work is done this time. Come on in. You can spend the day here. I might poke around a little, but I'm going to be mighty careful. I ain't sure Norrid won't sic that killer on me since he's already gotten rid of my pa."

"Maybe we'd both better stay holed up today," Paxton suggested.

Paxton did stay indoors most of the day. But he saw nobody pass the place, and Rooker saw no one on his two short scouting trips.

With the coming of night, Paxton headed for town again. Rooker insisted on going along although Paxton repeated that it wasn't his fight.

"Ain't many of us who fight only in our own wars," Rooker said. "Look how many got killed in the war fifteen years ago. I'll bet there wasn't many of them who had any personal fight in that."

Paxton couldn't argue that point. He didn't see how it had anything to do with Rooker helping Paxton look for his brother, but he let it ride. Rooker knew Monotony better than he did. He might know more hiding places.

They planned their arrival in town for an hour when most of the inhabitants were already in bed. Buskey never showed himself outside the pool hall after dark except to go home, so they had no fear of bumping into him. They poked into every barn and shed around town and even examined the backs of the business places, thinking there might be a cubbyhole or basement where Gary could be hiding.

Paxton had hopes of finding him when they checked the back of Horn's office. The door was unlocked and, striking a match, Paxton could see that someone had been staying there. But there was no one there now.

"Could have been his hideout," Rooker

said when they were back outside. "Doesn't look like it was used today, though. That just about covers the town. We'd better get home and get to bed ourselves."

"Go ahead," Paxton said. "Time is running out on me. I'm going to stick around and see if I can locate any clue. Something might show up."

"Not likely tonight," Rooker said. "Everybody has gone to bed."

"If Gary is hiding, he might come out to get the things he needs to live on. He'd be safer doing it after midnight than any other time. I'll stay and watch. You go on home."

Reluctantly, Rooker agreed. "You get out of here before the town starts waking up," he warned. "If you don't find Gary before then, it's a cinch you're not going to find him after the town starts stirring."

Rooker disappeared toward the spot where they'd left their horses. Paxton tried to fight down the growing conviction that his brother was already dead. He had searched the town and the caves along the creek without finding any trace of him unless that makeshift bunk in the back of the lawyer's office was his. He clung to the hope that perhaps Gary was out foraging right now and would return to the back room of the office.

Fading into the deep shadows near the corner of the lawyer's office, he waited. The town was quiet now; there were only a few lights, and they were all up on the bench above the main street of town. Some people hadn't gone to bed yet.

Paxton caught a sound on the far side of the office, and his hand dipped carefully to his gun and brought it up with his finger outside the trigger guard. If that was Gary, he didn't want to scare him. But if it was someone else, he had to be ready.

He waited tensely, his eyes straining to see into the dark alley. The sound came again, something like the scuffing of a boot on soft ground. Then he saw movement at the corner low to the ground. His heart felt as big as a bucket in his chest until he realized it was nothing but a dog sniffing the ground along the alley, apparently doing some foraging.

Paxton relaxed, realizing how tight his nerves had become while he was waiting to identify whatever was on the far side of the office. The dog, locating Paxton, bristled and growled softly but turned away behind the bank and continued sniffing his way over town.

Paxton got tired of waiting and decided to prowl around the hotel once more. The hotel was one of the biggest buildings in town even though it seemed doubtful that much of the building was ever used. Monotony had few visitors.

He kept his hand close to his gun as he walked softly. He felt almost as if he were in the enemy camp. Buskey and Norrid both had to be considered his enemies, and both were here in town. The lawyer over in the church might be called a friend, but he was little help in his condition.

Stepping around the rear corner of the hotel, he suddenly came face to face with a big man who evidently was prowling the same as Paxton was. Paxton's gun came into his hand almost involuntarily. That quickness had saved Paxton in tight spots before. It gave him the upper hand now.

The other man had his hand on his gun, but he pulled it away as if he had touched a hot stove. Paxton sized up the man. He was shorter than Paxton but thirty or forty pounds heavier.

"Are you going to shoot?" the man asked after a minute.

"According to who you are," Paxton said.

The man was slow in answering. "My name is Gary Wirth," he said finally.

Paxton suppressed his shock. He hadn't

expected his brother to look like this man. He was much bigger than he had thought Gary would be, and he seemed to slop over his clothes rather than fit into them. Paxton had always imagined that his brother, who was a schoolteacher in Texas, would be a neat dresser.

"Are you going to kill me?" the man repeated.

Paxton slowly put his gun away. "I'm Dave Paxton," he said. "I've been hunting this town over for you."

The other man grinned. "That's a relief. There are men here in town who are trying to kill me. I've been hiding most of the time. We've got to find the lawyer, Mark Horn, and get that inheritance settled."

Paxton nodded. The doubts that were prodding him faded a little. This surely must be Gary. Nobody else would know that the two brothers had to appear before Mark Horn to claim that inheritance. In fact, nobody else ought to know anything about the conditions of Joshua's will.

"Do you know where Horn is?" Paxton asked.

"No. But I figure you do. Let's go see him."

Paxton moved out from the deep shadow of the building and the other man followed. Paxton studied him again. The flabby face with the close set pig eyes; the bulging stomach and spindly legs; they just didn't fit Paxton's picture of Gary at all.

"We've got plenty of time," Paxton said, watching the man closely.

"October 4 isn't that far away."

Paxton nodded. This must be Gary. Who else would know about the deadline? "Horn is pretty well beaten up, but he is getting better. He's over in the church."

"Let's go talk to him."

Paxton stepped aside and let the big man take the lead down the length of the hotel to the street. At this time of night, the street was empty and dark. Together they walked across the street to the church. Paxton opened the door and they stepped inside.

The interior of the church was as black as a bottomless pit at midnight. Paxton stopped just a short distance inside the door. He couldn't be sure that Horn was still here.

"Mr. Horn," he called softly. "It's me, Dave Paxton."

"Over here," Horn said from the corner. "Did you find Gary?"

Paxton felt his way toward the lawyer, brushing his hand from one row of pews to the next as he went down the aisle.

"I found him," he said. "He's here with me."

"Where?" Horn asked.

"I'm right here," the big man said.

"You're not Gary!" Horn half screamed. "You're Yount!"

Horn couldn't see in the dark, but he could recognize voices. Paxton knew then why he hadn't felt like a brother to this big man.

His hand dropped to his gun. Just then the big man swung a fist at Paxton and in the dark hit his arm, sending his gun spinning away against the far wall. Yount was the only man in the church now with a gun.

Chapter 19

"You're not going to beat me out of what is mine!" Yount yelled.

Paxton couldn't see him, but he pinpointed his location by sound. Yount apparently had recognized Paxton or guessed who he was back at the hotel and had claimed to be Gary Wirth to save his skin. Then he had used Paxton to find Horn. Now he had them both at his mercy. He probably knew where Gary was or he wouldn't have been so confident in posing as Gary.

Paxton's hand came in contact with a song book on the front pew. He didn't stop to think how inadequate a song book was in fighting a six-gun. He threw the book with all his strength.

The book plopped solidly against its target. Yount swore as he staggered back. Paxton launched himself like a cougar at the sound. His only chance to neutralize that gun was to get so close that Yount couldn't use it.

He hit the big man as he was trying to recover his balance. Paxton's weight carried them both to the floor. Paxton grabbed Yount's arm to keep him from clawing his gun out of the holster. He wished he had his own gun now. If ever a man deserved killing, it was Yount, considering the way he had beaten up Mark Horn. No telling what he had done to Gary.

Yount tried to twist free, but Paxton hammered his fist into Yount's face, feeling the slickness of the blood that spurted from his nose. Yount suddenly erupted with all his strength and upset Paxton.

Before Paxton could recover, the big man had rolled free and was scrambling up the aisle. Paxton went after him, but bumped hard into a pew. It sent him reeling, and by the time he had righted himself, Yount was charging out the front door. Maybe Yount didn't know that Paxton had lost his gun. It would explain why he had run instead of staying to fight.

Paxton considered going after him but quickly discarded that idea. Yount still had his gun; Paxton didn't. Out in the street, the advantage would be Yount's. He turned to the wall where his gun had skidded when Yount had knocked it out of his hand. Feeling along the floor, he searched for several minutes but couldn't find it. He dared not strike a match. Yount might be watching at a window.

He called for Mrs. Fenton, and she answered immediately from the far side of the church. "We'll have to move Mr. Horn now," he said. "That man wants to kill him."

"That's right," Horn agreed with more strength than Paxton had expected him to have. "He knows what I'll do to him if I ever get him in court. At first, he thought I'd turn the land over to him if you and Gary didn't meet the terms of the will. But he's gone too far for that now. He may get the land but never by my hand. He has to get rid of me."

"Where can we take him?" Mrs. Fenton asked.

"How about your place? Would anyone look there?"

"Not likely," she said. "But it's quite a ways from here."

"I'll carry Mr. Horn," Paxton said. "Lead the way."

"Shouldn't we wait till we're sure that man is gone?" Mrs. Fenton asked.

"He'll come nearer finding us if we stay here than if we move," Paxton said. "I'll make sure he's gone now."

He went to pick up Horn but found that he could walk slowly with help. That would certainly be better than carrying him. He was a heavy man.

At the door, Paxton stopped the other two while he moved outside. He was tense, ready to dive back inside. If Yount was watching, he'd go for Paxton. He was the one he wanted; he could get to Horn easily once Paxton was out of the way. But there was no sound outside.

Paxton stepped back inside. "He seems to be gone. Let's move while we can. He's sure to come back."

They went outside, Horn leaning heavily on Paxton. Mrs. Fenton turned back along the side of the church then went behind the business places, moving past the millinery shop, the drugstore and the blacksmith shop. When she reached the corral behind the livery barn, she turned toward the street, hugging the front of the livery then cutting across the street to the feed store. She paused beside the feed store to let Mark Horn rest. He'd gone about as far as he could without a stop.

"We're almost there," Mrs. Fenton said. "I live up on the next street, but it's quite a climb."

After a short rest, they continued,

climbing up to the next bench above the creek. Paxton was glad when Mrs. Fenton motioned them up a walk to the door of a house. Inside, they made Horn comfortable in a big bed.

Tired as he was, Horn wanted to talk. "I'm sure Gary is around town," he said to Paxton. "He was in to see me shortly after you were the other night. Wanted to know where you were."

"What did you tell him?"

"That I thought you were up the Cottonwood, probably staying with Jeff Rooker. He said he'd look there for you."

"If he'd found Rooker, I'd have known about it," Paxton said. "Something must have happened to him."

"Yount probably caught him."

"Do you think he might have killed him?"

"I doubt it. He'd rather have you dead than Gary. He knows that Gary won't fight back if he gets the land, but you will. So he has to get rid of you, or he'll never be able to own that land."

"You can lay odds on that," Paxton said savagely. "I've got to find my gun and go after Yount before he does any more damage."

He started toward the door, but Mrs.

Fenton stopped him. "Stay till morning," she begged.

He sighed. Maybe he couldn't find his gun in the dark. Yount might be back at the church by now waiting for Paxton to show up. He had to be careful, until he got his gun. A gunfighter without a gun was worse than a bird without feathers. At least he'd recognize Yount the next time he saw him.

As soon as breakfast was over, Paxton slipped out the back door of Mrs. Fenton's house and made his way down the alleys toward the main part of town and the church. The first man he saw was the preacher, Sutcliffe, coming out of the church. He had evidently come to see how Mark Horn was doing. Paxton caught his attention, and Sutcliffe came to the alley where Paxton waited.

"Where did you take the lawyer?" Sutcliffe demanded, stepping off the street.

Paxton explained. Then he asked if Sutcliffe had a gun he could borrow just in case he couldn't find his own.

"I don't use a gun," Sutcliffe said in an offended tone.

"Didn't figure you for a gunfighter," Paxton said. "But I'm going to need a gun to survive."

"There has to be a better way to survive," Sutcliffe said. "Perhaps Bertha can help you."

"How? Is she calling on the spirits again?"

"She's always trying to help people. She has agreed to hold another seance soon. Perhaps she can get some answers for you then."

"I need the answers now. I also need a gun now. Can she call that up for me?"

"The spirits do not condone violence," Sutcliffe chided gently. "Their messages are of great value to us mortals."

"From what I hear, a lot of people got the message when that ghost on the white horse came through the grove the other night," Paxton said, trying not to grin.

"That was a most dramatic appearance," Sutcliffe said solemnly. "Bertha will not hold her next seance in the grove, however. It may be at my home."

"Have you seen Caleb Yount this morning?"

"I came in to see Mr. Horn," Sutcliffe said. "Who is Caleb Yount?"

"He's a heavyset man, not too tall but tipping the scales in the neighborhood of a fat hog ready for market."

"I did see a rather plump man as I rode in."

"Where was he?"

"Heading toward the creek," Sutcliffe said. "Is he someone I should know?"

"He's the one who beat up the lawyer. Are there any caves along the creek close to town?"

"A couple," Sutcliffe said. "Both of them are just above the grove."

Paxton remembered the cave he'd found that looked as if it had been lived in. Maybe that was Yount's hideout. Making sure no one was in the street, he left Sutcliffe and crossed quickly to the church. Stepping inside, he went to the wall where the gun had been knocked from his hand. It wasn't very light inside, but it was light enough to reveal a gun if it was there.

A five-minute search turned up nothing. The only answer, he decided, was that Yount had come back to finish the job he'd aborted after Paxton knocked him down, and finding no one there, he had located the gun and taken it to make sure Paxton would be unarmed the next time they met.

Going outside, he ducked down the side of the church toward the creek. He had a rifle on the saddle on his old black horse.

He and Rooker had left their horses close to the creek last night. The horse was gone, however. He was afoot and unarmed. But he had a line on Yount's whereabouts if Sutcliffe had been right in identifying Yount. If Gary was still alive, he likely was being held wherever Yount was holed up.

He couldn't wait to find another gun. He wouldn't crowd his luck, but he would try to find out whether Yount was using one of those caves as a hideout.

Turning upstream, he went through the cottonwood grove and aimed at the bluffs a short distance away. This section of bluffs stretched along the creek for a quarter of a mile. He found a cave shortly after reaching them. It was on the same level as the ones farther upstream.

Seeing and hearing nothing, Paxton moved inside cautiously. He wanted to find Gary if he was being held a prisoner, but without a gun, he didn't want to find Yount. Sutcliffe had seen Yount earlier this morning, but Yount might be anywhere now.

Moving slowly forward, giving his eyes time to adjust to the dim light he saw that the cave was big enough for a man to live in. He even saw signs that someone had been there recently. He advanced more cautiously.

When he reached the point where he could no longer see, he stopped and listened intently. The darkness and silence were eerie, especially when he knew that Yount might be waiting for him just a few feet ahead.

Finally, hearing nothing, he called Gary's name softly. The sound whispered through the cave. He called louder. There was still no answer. If Gary was in here, he'd have made some sound even if he was gagged. But that was no guarantee that Caleb Yount wasn't there, still waiting.

He couldn't see to go farther. Striking a match would be inviting a bullet if Yount was here. He turned back to the mouth of the cave. If Yount was in the cave, he'd surely make his move now and not let Paxton get out. There was still no sound behind him. Paxton at last let his nerves relax. The cave was obviously empty.

Reaching the mouth of the cave, he waited until his eyes adjusted back to the sunlight shining against the bluffs. He stepped outside, and a shower of rock dust slapped him in the face. The echo of the shot came as he was diving back into the mouth of the cave. Someone had been waiting until he came out.

He spotted the ambusher's rock off to

the right. He controlled the area where Paxton had intended to go. His eyes ran over the cave opening. There was a rock on the other side of the cave mouth that had tumbled down from the bluff in ages past. If he could get behind that, he might slip away into the gully beyond the cave. It was his only chance. With no gun, he couldn't fight back. Once the ambusher was sure he had no gun, he'd move in quickly for the kill.

Backtracking, he crossed to the other side of the cave and moved forward. There was one place where he had to lie flat and wriggle ahead like a snake. But he made it to the rock. There was a two-foot-wide passage behind the rock and some choke-cherry bushes just behind. Squirming through the narrow passage, he got into the chokecherries. They tore at his clothes, but he worked his way carefully through them, trying not to make any movement that the man down on the creek could see.

At last, he came to the gully that led back up through the bluff to the top. That wasn't where he wanted to go but he had no other choice. At the top of the bluff, he peered over the edge. He dropped like a rock. Tug Buskey was coming on the run, apparently attracted by the sound of that shot.

Keeping low, Paxton waited until Buskey disappeared over the edge of the bluff toward the creek. Then he rose to a crouch and sprinted up the gully. He could see that it was leading him right to town which he didn't like. But it was away from the marksman and Buskey.

He'd have a hard time getting out of town, but it appeared to be the safest place for him right now. With no gun, he didn't dare be caught out on the open prairie.

The gully ended a short distance from the livery barn. He ran for the barn and climbed into the corral. As he did, he heard a yell back toward the grove. Buskey had spotted him. Dashing into the barn, he thought of taking a horse. But the owner was there, glaring at him. He didn't have time to explain or fight the man for a horse. He ran on through the barn and dodged across to the feed store, past the jail and Buskey's office, and on toward the homes on the second bench above the creek. Seeing the barn behind Norrid's house, he decided on that.

Norrid had a big barn with four two-horse stalls. There were three horses in the barn and one in the corral now. Paxton dived into an empty stall. The manger was almost full of hay and Paxton worked his way down into the hay. It was the best he could do. He couldn't fight guns with fists.

He listened for the searchers, but they didn't come. They must have thought he had stopped at the livery barn or had gone some other direction.

Then Norrid came to the barn for his team of horses. Paxton braced himself for discovery. Norrid wasn't likely to overlook him. He would be armed, and he wanted Paxton dead as much as anyone in Monotony.

Chapter 20

Elias Norrid's mind was far from what he was doing when he came into the barn. This trip for Bertha was absolutely unnecessary, the way he saw it. Bertha was determined to go, however, and Norrid wasn't sure how much he dared cross her.

He didn't believe in her seances, yet she had been right in so many of her predictions that it was almost uncanny. She had threatened that if he didn't do what she asked, the spirits would do dire things to him. After all he had seen and heard recently, he wasn't at all sure that she wouldn't be right in that too.

Norrid grabbed a collar and slid in beside one of the horses he used on the buggy. If Bertha would just wait, Sutcliffe would likely come to town. She could talk to him then and save this whole trip. Maybe he was in town today. That thought brightened Norrid's outlook a little. But if he went to town to see if Sutcliffe was there, Bertha would be furious. She had sent him to get the buggy to take her out to Sutcliffe's. He'd better do it. No telling what kind of curse she'd put on him if he didn't.

He got the harness and slapped it on the horse and buckled it in place. Then he got the collar and harness on the other horse. Maybe Bertha would ask the spirits if there really was any money buried at the spring. That possibility nagged him constantly. He hadn't found any proof that there was any money there. Yet there were so many looking for it that there had to be something to it. He'd make Bertha ask the spirits about the money. He knew how to do it.

He started to back the team out of the stall when he thought he heard a noise in the next stall. That couldn't be. That stall was empty. He stared over the partition for a moment, then shrugged and backed the horses into the runway. Leading them to the buggy in the lean-to shed, he backed them into place, lifted the yoke and snapped it to the breast straps under the collars.

He heard the sound again, and this time, he knew there was no mistake. Reaching into the front of the buggy where he always kept a rifle, he lifted it out and turned toward the empty stall. The deputy sheriff, Tug Buskey, came puffing around the corner just then.

"Have you seen that fellow we thought we burned out in that log house along the creek?" he demanded.

Norrid felt the queasy feeling welling up in his stomach like it did every time he heard that man mentioned. "You mean that ghost?" he asked, hesitating even to say the word.

"He didn't look like no ghost to me," Buskey snorted. "He's here in town somewhere. He won't get away. I'll flush him out and see if he bleeds when he's shot."

"I haven't seen him. I'd have shot him if I had." Norrid tapped his rifle.

"I'm going to look in your barn anyway," Buskey said. "A fellow named Yount is helping me look. We'll get him."

Buskey disappeared inside the barn and came out again about the time Norrid finished hooking the tugs to the buggy. Norrid climbed into the buggy and drove around to the front of the big house.

Before Bertha came out of the house, Yount came running up from the direction of the hotel.

"Have you seen Paxton?"

"Paxton?" Norrid repeated.

"Sure. The guy who is a shirttail relative of Joshua Greer. He could inherit the land you took away from Greer."

"I didn't take any land from Greer. Greer stole my spring."

He glared at Yount. He didn't like him, but he seemed to know more than a stranger ought to know. And he was after Paxton, Joshua Greer's foster nephew. That made him an ally whether Norrid liked it or not.

"I almost got him in the church last night," Yount said. "Had him dead to rights. Then he threw something and knocked me down. I was lucky to get out alive."

"I wish you had gotten him," Norrid said.

"I'll get him. We've told the livery man what will happen to him if he lets him have a horse. We'll see that nobody else gives him one. Even if he got a horse, he'd never get out of town." He turned and moved off at a lumbering trot.

So it was Paxton they had burned in that house; at least, they thought they had. That answered all the questions except why he was still running around.

Norrid was satisfied that Buskey and Yount would keep the town buttoned up so tight that Paxton could not get out. He looked so much like Kucek that it was frightening. But he knew now that he wasn't Kucek. Maybe he was a ghost. If so, then Buskey and Yount were wasting their time trying to corral him. If Paxton was the man he'd seen on that white horse, he was either a ghost or he had nine lives like a cat.

As long as he had to go to Sutcliffe's, maybe he should go on to the Circle N and talk to Kucek. If Kucek wanted to earn his money, he could come to town and search out Paxton himself. He had the feeling that if Paxton wasn't a ghost, he'd still be hiding somewhere here in town by the time he got word to Kucek.

Bertha came waddling out of the house and climbed heavily into the buggy. Norrid thought sourly that she almost upset the buggy when she put her weight on the little iron step on the side.

As he drove to the main street, Norrid considered how he could use a man like Caleb Yount on his payroll. He was about as determined as anyone he ever saw. Determination was half the battle of winning.

In front of the general store, Norrid yelled for Upshaw, and the fat storekeeper came to the door. Norrid asked if Sutcliffe was in town. When he heard that he had been here but had gone home an hour ago, Norrid's disgust grew. He could have saved this trip if he'd only known.

Slapping the lines over the horses' backs, he drove out of town. He glared over at Bertha, holding his silence until they reached the first bluffs.

"Are you going to have another seance?"

Bertha nodded. "That's what I'm going to talk to Mr. Sutcliffe about."

"You can just ask those spirits if there is any money buried at that spring," he growled.

"I will not!" Bertha snapped indignantly. "We do not use the spirits for anything mercenary."

Norrid had timed his question with precision. They were driving along the top of the highest bluff close to town. He glanced over at Bertha. She was deathly afraid of high places. He pulled the team toward the edge of the bluff. Bertha started to yell at him. Then her yell turned to a scream of terror. Norrid stopped the horses.

"Are you going to ask the spirits to locate that money for me?"

Bertha tried to speak but her eyes were glued to the edge of the bluff. Finally she just nodded.

Norrid turned the team back to the road. He'd made her promise, but he knew he really hadn't gained anything. Bertha was not one to be bullied into doing things. How was he to know that what she told him was what the spirits had told her?

Bertha refused to say a word all the rest of the way to Sutcliffe's. Maybe he had pushed her too far, but he didn't care if she thought he was acting like a spoiled child. He had important things to do — far more important than driving her all over the country. The least she could do was help him a little.

When they reached Sutcliffe's, the preacher came out to the buggy and helped Bertha get down. Norrid said he'd be back later to pick her up, and he drove off without even telling Bertha where he was going. Let her stew, he thought.

It was only a little out of his way to stop at the spring on his way from Sutcliffe's to the Circle N. He wanted to make sure nobody had done any digging after he'd been there.

He found that there had been a lot of digging, and his anger grew. Loanda was there, which was a surprise in itself. She seemed cool as ice water about it. It was like trying to keep rabbits out of a garden, she said. This was a bit more important than a garden, the way Norrid saw it.

He slapped the lines angrily and drove on to the Circle N. He'd light a fire under Tidrow and Kucek to get this digging stopped.

He saw Kucek loafing at the corral when he drove into the yard at the Circle N, and he headed his team that way.

"Thought I hired you to do a job for me," he said angrily.

"I'm doing it," Kucek said. He came over and leaned against the front wheel of the buggy. "I'm sure that this ghost of yours is really Dave Paxton."

Norrid nodded. "I've figured that out myself. But he may be more of a ghost than you think. Nobody seems to be able to kill him even when they're at pointblank range."

Kucek didn't seem ruffled. "I found out that Paxton has one thing in mind. He's here to get revenge on the men who helped kill Joshua and Roy Greer."

"That gives you an added reason for getting rid of him," Norrid said. "You killed them."

"He ain't after just the one who did the shooting. He's after every man who had a part in it. That means especially the one who paid the bill."

Norrid shifted uneasily. He didn't like to have things like that brought out in open conversation. That kind of bargain should never see the light of day.

"He'll still be after the man who shot them," Norrid said.

"Of course," Kucek agreed. "But he's not going to crowd me. Nobody crowds me and lives. But it might be different with the man who paid the money. Can you face him with a gun?"

"He won't come looking for me till he gets you," Norrid said, trying to sound confident.

"Don't lay odds on that. Now that I see what I'm up against, I'm going to need more money for this job."

Fury pushed the fear out of Norrid. "We made a deal," he snapped. "That's it!"

Kucek shrugged and backed away from the wheel. "Then I'll be riding on. Paxton ain't going to follow me."

Panic hit Norrid. If Kucek was right about Paxton being here for revenge, and it was more than likely that he was, then Norrid would be at the head of his list if Kucek left. Paxton was trapped in town right now. But that really didn't mean much. He'd been trapped in tighter spots than that and walked off untouched.

"I might even take some of your money from the bank when I go," Kucek added.

Norrid almost choked. He could probably do that, too. Who was there who could stop him? Not even Ortis was good enough with a gun to handle Kucek. Kucek held a handful of aces, and Norrid felt like his highest card was a deuce.

"All right," he said finally. "Double what I promised."

Kucek nodded. "That's more like it."

Norrid saw Tidrow over by another corral, and he slapped the lines on his team, moving away from Kucek. He felt like he was escaping from the smell of death.

"I want you to get all the boys together that you can spare," he told Tidrow. "Bring them to town as soon as you can. Buskey has Paxton trapped in town. I want you to come in and help get him."

"Is Paxton the ghost?"

Norrid nodded, hating that word. "A man named Yount is helping Buskey search the town for Paxton now. They're making sure that he doesn't get out of town. With your men, you can dig him out."

"I have to go to town for a load of salt anyway," Tidrow said. "I figured on doing it tomorrow. I'll just hitch up and go in today. We've got most of the boys right close to the ranch too. I'll send Al out after them."

"Good," Norrid said. "I want to make sure that Paxton does not get out of this trap."

"If we can't hit him any better than we did the other night at the spring, all the men in the country couldn't get him."

"He can be hit," Norrid said sharply. "Don't even think that he can't."

"If that is Paxton, and maybe it is, then we've all got a stake in getting rid of him," Tidrow said. "Shall I bring Kucek?"

"Be sure to bring him," Norrid said. "Paxton is the one I hired him to kill. I want to make sure he does something to earn his money."

Norrid slapped the lines again and wheeled the buggy out of the yard. He headed back to Sutcliffe's. Likely Bertha was standing on her ear waiting for him. If she couldn't understand that he had more on his mind than her silly seances, then she'd just have to blow her top.

Bertha was waiting, but she was too excited about the seance she and Sutcliffe had planned at Sutcliffe's place to rant about his being late. Norrid drove back to town in silence, lost in thought. Even after Paxton was gone, would Kucek leave? He had mentioned the money in Norrid's bank. Wasn't he likely to take that when he left? What was there to stop him? If Norrid raised too big a stink, Kucek might tell everybody that Norrid had hired him to kill three men. How had he gotten into so much trouble when he thought he had it all worked out?

Maybe Yount would be a help, but he doubted it — not against a man like Kucek. The money at the spring had somehow lost its importance. It would be a small consolation if Kucek got the money in the bank.

He put the team away after letting Bertha out at the front door. His hands trembled as he worked with the harness. It had not been a good day for him.

Chapter 21

Dave Paxton had heard Norrid coming with the team and buggy and had slipped back into the manger full of hay. He waited quietly, hoping Norrid wouldn't find him. He might decide to feed the hay from this manger to the horses. He could imagine the tines of a fork probing into the hay and hitting him.

Norrid finished unharnessing the horses, however, and turned them out into the little corral behind the barn to roll and get a drink at the trough. He heard Norrid mumbling to himself as he went through the barn door toward the house. Something was bothering the banker more than usual.

Sure that Norrid was gone, Paxton crawled out of the manger again. Moving to the door, he looked down toward town. Upshaw was still out behind his store as if he was sure he'd see Paxton from there. Paxton wondered how he'd feel if he knew how close he was to him.

Either Upshaw or Yount or Buskey had been in sight of the barn most of the day. Paxton had planned to take the saddle horse that Norrid had in the barn and make a dash for it. But every time he thought he had a chance, one of the men showed up out there. If he'd had a gun, he'd have taken his chances on shooting his way through. But he was unarmed and those men had both revolvers and rifles. When it got dark, he could slip out. Nobody had found him here yet, and they weren't liable to now.

Paxton saw Icky Minton out behind the hotel. That was not so unusual because he lived in the cellar under the hotel. But he kept wandering around. He wasn't doing any of the chores the hotel had hired him to do. He didn't go near Upshaw, and finally he disappeared from Paxton's view.

Paxton continued to watch Upshaw, although now he had decided to wait for darkness. The risk of detection was too great if he took the saddle horse and made a break. Darkness would give him a better chance.

Suddenly, almost as if he had appeared out of the ground, Icky bobbed into the barn. Paxton had been watching Upshaw and hadn't seen Icky come up from the other side.

"What are you going here, Icky?" Paxton demanded when he had swallowed his surprise.

"Came to see you," Icky said.

"How did you know I was here?"

Icky shrugged. "Mr. Norrid has two saddle horses beside the buggy team. When one horse is in the corral and the other one is here, the one in the corral keeps coming to the barn door. Today it didn't. I figured something was in here it didn't like. I decided it was you since Tug and Yount had looked in all of the houses in town without finding you."

Paxton wondered how anybody could consider Icky a dummy. Then another thought hit him. "Did they find Horn?"

Icky shook his head. "Mrs. Fenton piled some quilts on the bed over Mr. Horn when they came and said she was patching them."

"Are you going to tell them you found me?"

"Only Jeff Rooker," Icky said. "He's down close to the bank now. But he wants to meet you behind Upshaw's store when there is nobody watching."

"When's that going to be?" Paxton growled. "Somebody's been watching all day."

"I'll keep an eye on everybody. When they're all away from the store, I'll let you know."

Icky ducked out of the barn and disappeared. He showed up again after a couple of minutes behind the hotel. Upshaw went into the store. Maybe a customer had called him in. Paxton watched for Rooker and finally saw him over behind the bank. Icky disappeared again toward the front of the hotel. Checking on the location of the searchers, Paxton guessed. Surely Buskey and Yount had lost some of their enthusiasm for the search by now.

Upshaw returned to the back of the store but only to draw the door closed from the inside. Rooker moved across the street to the rear of the general store. Still none of the searchers showed up.

Icky bobbed in again without Paxton seeing him come. "You can make it now," he said. "Upshaw went down to the pool hall. He'll be there for an hour drinking before he goes home. Yount has just disappeared."

Paxton looked at his watch. It was four o'clock. Too early for Upshaw to be closing his store for the day. But Icky had the uncanny ability to know what each man in town would do. Paxton wasn't going to argue with him.

"Something else," Icky said. "Sam Tidrow has brought in all the Circle N hands. They're spreading out around the town."

"What for?" Paxton asked, guessing why before he heard the answer. He had waited too long.

"Reckon they heard you were cornered in town, and they've come to help smoke you out. Buskey and Mr. Norrid have gone up to talk to Tidrow near the grove. This is your chance to get down to the store."

"Will I be any better off there than I am here?"

"You'll have Rooker to help you," Icky said.

Paxton nodded, knowing he was going to need all the help he could get. He wished he had tried a break earlier in the day. There had been only three men to dodge then. Now there was all the Circle N. He had no idea how many men that would be. Far too many, that was sure.

"All right," he agreed. "I'll get down there as fast as I can."

Icky slipped out the way he had come. Paxton checked again to see that no one was in sight at the rear of the store buildings. Someone in one of the houses up here on the second bench might see him.

243

But that was a chance he had to take.

He tried to walk nonchalantly toward the store, but he could almost feel eyes on him. He moved faster and faster. Rooker had seen him and was waiting by the rear door of the store.

"This back door isn't locked," Rooker said softly when Paxton reached him. "Let's get inside."

He opened the door, and they stepped into the rear room which was full of sacks and barrels and boxes. He handed Paxton a gun after glancing at his empty holster.

"Perhaps this might come in handy."

"I've felt undressed all day without one," Paxton said. He dropped the gun in his holster.

"Someone's coming now," Rooker said suddenly. "You can hide among those sacks."

Paxton dropped down behind a pile of sacks. He was getting mighty tired of hiding all the time. That wasn't the way he liked to fight his battles. Then he heard Icky's voice and stood up.

"They've got the whole town sur-rounded," Icky reported. "Tidrow brought more than a dozen men. Along with what they have here already. They've got enough to keep a fly from getting out of town."

"What are they going to do now?" Rooker asked.

"Search the town, house to house, the way I get it. They are sure that Mr. Paxton is here, and they're going to get him."

Paxton considered his chances. If he did anything, it would have to be immediately. They'd soon close in until a snake couldn't slip through. He thought of dashing through with his gun blazing. But he didn't even have a horse.

A wagon rumbled down the alley to the back of the store. Icky disappeared like a shadow and Rooker went into the front part of the store. Paxton sank down behind the pile of sacks. If this was the enemy and they found him, at least, he'd have a gun and make a fight of it.

Peeking out over the sacks, he saw a man open the rear door and Sam Tidrow back a wagon up to it. Upshaw came from the front of the store. Apparently, he had been rousted out of the pool hall.

"I need about three barrels of salt," Tidrow said. "I'm going to leave my wagon here till we find Paxton. I'll load the salt then."

"I've got lots of salt," Upshaw said. "Need me to help hunt?"

"Need every man we can get," Tidrow

said. "We're going to find him if he's still in town."

"He's here," Upshaw declared and went down the back alley with Tidrow.

Paxton got out from behind the pile of sacks. His situation was getting worse. They'd search this storeroom and they'd find him among those sacks. Going toward the door, he bumped into a salt barrel and an idea struck him. He moved among the barrels, thumping them. Near the partition door, he found one that sounded hollow. The lid was off and it was almost empty. Upshaw must have been selling small quantities out of this barrel.

Quickly Paxton upended the barrel and drained the remaining salt out on the floor behind some boxes. He found the lid to the barrel which had been pried off in one piece. He set the barrel up close to the partition where it had been. Rooker came through the store to the back room.

"I'll need some help here," Paxton said. "They're going to take this room apart before they're through so I'm going to turn into a barrel of salt."

"Salt?" Rooker exclaimed. "Are you crazy? You're going to turn into a corpse."

"They won't kill me if they can't see me. I'll get into this barrel. You nail the lid on."

"That's going to be a mighty tight fit."

"It's better than facing ten guns," Paxton said.

"I hear they're after salt," Rooker said. "They might take your barrel."

"This barrel is over here away from the others. They're not likely to touch it."

Rooker was still hesitating when they heard men coming down the alley. Paxton squeezed himself into the barrel with his gun pointed up right beside his head. Rooker nailed the lid on, leaving it slightly loose so Paxton could breathe. If the barrel had been a half inch smaller, he wouldn't have been able to squeeze in.

"Look everywhere," Paxton heard one man yell. "We've been through every store and house and barn in town. This is the last place where he could be."

Paxton could hear things being shifted around. There was a lot of grumbling because they hadn't found Paxton. Finally one man ordered the others to load the three barrels of salt they had bought.

Somebody was beside Paxton's barrel right then, and he tipped the barrel over where it landed with a thud. Then it was rolled across the floor and heaved into the wagon.

"That's mighty heavy salt," one man growled.

"Salt ain't feathers," another man said.

There was more thumping as the other barrels were lifted in. Then the wagon began moving. The swaying and bumping almost made Paxton sick. He was glad they had set the barrels on end rather than letting them roll back and forth over the wagon.

Even over the noise created by the barrels bouncing in the wagon, Paxton heard the men grumbling about not finding their man.

"Upshaw said he couldn't possibly have gotten out of town," one man, apparently the driver of the wagon, said sharply. "He must have dug a hole and crawled into it then pulled it in after him."

"A lot of people say he's a ghost," another man said. "Maybe he just walked right through us, and we didn't even see him."

"I wish you'd shut up about ghosts," another said from the other side of the wagon.

Paxton realized that there were Circle N riders moving along on either side of the wagon. How was he going to get out of this barrel without being killed? He could only hope they'd unload the barrels and leave them until tomorrow before opening them.

"I don't like ghosts no better than you do," the first man yelled back across the wagon. "But you know how many people have tried to kill this one, and nobody has drawn blood yet."

"Ghosts don't bleed," another chimed in.

"Shut up, will you?" one man yelled. "We ain't dealing with no ghost. He just gave us the slip somehow."

The wagon jolted on, but the men stopped talking. Paxton felt his bruises getting bigger as the barrel bounced and rocked against the others. If he got out of the barrel, he wasn't sure he could move his muscles. He had wanted to get out of town, but it hadn't been his idea to have the Circle N take him out.

Finally, the team stopped and men climbed into the wagon, handing the barrels down to others on the ground. Paxton heard the wagon roll away as his barrel sat still for the first time in a long while. Now he had to get out of the barrel. Then he heard voices. Someone was still here.

"Sam says we've got to open one barrel and put out some salt tonight," one man said.

"Let's shoot the barrel full of holes and let the salt run out," another suggested.

"We didn't get to shoot at nothing in town."

Paxton gripped his gun, but it wouldn't do him any good if they decided to puncture the barrel with bullets. It was a typical stunt of frustrated ranch hands. They might pick one of the other barrels. But Paxton couldn't hope to be that lucky.

If they started shooting or even if they had guns in their hands when he broke open the lid, he wouldn't have a chance.

Chapter 22

All was quiet, and Paxton braced himself for a lunge upward, hoping the nails Rooker had driven into the barrel to hold the lid in place weren't too solid. Rooker hadn't pounded them all the way in, he knew.

"I'm tired," one man said. "Let's get this salt out for the critters and get in to supper."

"I've got a hammer. I'll break in a barrel top."

Paxton relaxed a bit. They were not going to shoot a barrel full of holes. He heard men walking around close to his barrel. Holding his gun high and hoping his fingers would work if he needed them, he ducked his head down. If they smashed the top of his barrel, the splintered board and maybe the hammer might come down far enough to hit him.

"Which one?" a voice asked.

"Don't make no difference," another said. "Salt's salt."

Paxton braced himself. He wondered

how many men he'd face when he got out of the barrel. He heard only the two voices the last few minutes. Maybe the rest had already left. The odds would be all against him even with two. He'd be stiffer than a dead cottonwood limb. He'd never been in such an uncomfortable place.

The hammer fell, and the barrel top split in half, caving in under the blow. Neither the wood nor the hammer hit Paxton. He pushed himself up out of the barrel with all his might.

One glance told him there were only two men here. It was deep twilight already. He'd had no idea of the passing of time while he was in that barrel. He pried his arms away from his side as he rose above the top of the barrel. The two men stared at him as if paralyzed. Then one broke for the house, dropping the hammer and yelling at the top of his lungs.

"Ghost! Ghost! The ghost's in the barrel!"

The other man backed off a step then stopped. Paxton recognized him then. Al Zamora. He hadn't been completely convinced of the ghost story from the first.

After the first shock, Zamora dug for his gun. Paxton already had his gun in his hand, but his arm and hand felt useless.

He brought the gun around in line with Zamora as Zamora fired. Even at that range, Zamora missed. Maybe it was his haste or the darkness or just plain fear.

Paxton had the gun in line, and he tensed his muscles to squeeze the trigger. The gun roared and Zamora was driven backward. Zamora fired again, but Paxton lunged forward, upsetting the barrel. He was sprawled out on the ground, half in and half out of the barrel like a hatching chicken. Zamora's shot went wild, and he didn't fire any more.

Paxton pulled himself out of the barrel as quickly as possible. The first man's yelling and these shots would bring the entire Circle N crew on the run.

Once on his feet, Paxton found that he could move although he ran like a spavined rooster. He barely glanced at Zamora as he passed him. His one shot had been enough.

By the time Paxton reached the corral, men were pouring out of the house and bunkhouse. Paxton had the use of his legs again, but he was still stiff. This violent exercise was taking the kinks out of muscles in a hurry.

There was general confusion among the men as they raced out to the spot where the salt barrels had been unloaded. Apparently, no one had seen Paxton run from there.

Paxton found a gentle horse close to the gate that allowed him to catch him. Grabbing a bridle from a post near the gate, he bridled the animal and swung the gate open. Throwing himself astride the bare-backed animal, he kicked his heels into his ribs, and the horse hit a gallop through the gate.

The men near the salt barrels heard the racket and wheeled, guns blazing. Bending low over the horse, Paxton soon got out of range of the men without being hit. The firing excited the other horses, and finding the gate open, they began charging through the gate to freedom.

Behind him, Paxton heard the men screaming and cursing. Glancing back in the early evening dusk, he saw them racing to close the gate. They'd keep some of the horses in the corral, but most were already gone. It was likely that the best horses were in the vanguard of the escape. They'd be the ones that were the fastest and strongest.

Paxton let the horse have his head and didn't realize, until he was halfway to the spring, just where he was headed. The road to town or to Rooker's was to the right, but Paxton let the horse go on toward the spring. If Loanda didn't shoot him for an intruder, this might be the safest place he could find. They surely wouldn't expect him to go to the spring.

He had no time to make a cautious approach. He let the horse thunder into the yard. When he pulled him to a halt, he faced Loanda with a rifle trained on him.

"Horse stealing now?" she demanded coldly.

"Didn't have time to get my own," Paxton said. "I just borrowed the only one I could catch."

"You would be able to catch Trinket anywhere," she said. "That's my horse. He's been down on the Circle N for a week."

"He just left the Circle N in a hurry," Paxton said. "I figure somebody may be coming to look for him."

Loanda nodded. "What kind of trouble did you have there?"

"Well, when they broke open the barrel and I popped out, Zamora tried to gun me down. He missed; I didn't."

"Popped out of a barrel?" she exclaimed, Then she cocked an ear. "They're coming." She stared at Paxton, her rifle still trained on him. Suddenly she lowered the gun as she reached her decision.

"Get inside. I'll turn Trinket into the corral. He is my horse."

Paxton slid off the horse and ran past Loanda into the house. Loanda led the horse into the corral, slipped off the bridle, and turned him loose. She was back at the house with Paxton hidden in the kitchen when the horses pulled up out front.

"Have you seen a jasper riding one of our horses?" a man yelled.

"I haven't seen one of your horses on this place till you rode in just now," she said. "Who are you looking for?"

"That ghost," one man said. "We brought three barrels of salt from town, and when we popped one open, this ghost jumped up. Shot Zamora and killed him. Al shot twice and never touched him. He took one of our horses and came this way."

"Sounds exciting," Loanda said calmly. "When will you learn that you can't shoot a ghost?"

"He can sure shoot us," the man said. "Vic, look over those horses in the corral."

Paxton waited, tense, gun ready. But the man came back to report that all the horses in the corral were Loanda's. Paxton relaxed.

"Must have gone on toward town," one man said. "Let's get going."

"Don't let the ghost get you," Loanda called after them.

Paxton was sure he heard some swearing above the clatter of hoofs. Then they were gone, and he came out of the kitchen.

"I owe you again for keeping the hounds off my trail."

"I didn't have time to think things out," Loanda said. "They were too close."

"Would you have turned me over to them if you'd had time to think?"

"I usually am satisfied with my snap decisions," she said. "Let's just say that I'm having fun with this ghost business. I can't let my ghost get killed."

"Got any extra grub? This ghost is about starved."

"When did you eat last?"

"Yesterday sometime. It's been so long, I lost track."

"I'll get something ready," Loanda said. "A starved ghost is almost as bad as one that won't bleed."

Paxton moved back from the light. Some Circle N rider might come back or a late one come here looking for those who had gone ahead.

"Does Elias Norrid run everything on

the Circle N?" he asked as she heated up the stove again which was still warm from cooking her own supper.

"Not just the Circle N. He runs about everything in the country, including Monotony. He owns the bank and half the country owes him money. What he says goes."

"You don't sound like you think much of the way he runs things."

"I didn't say that," she said quickly. "He sort of runs over anything that doesn't get out of his way. He did put me here on this land, and I'm most grateful for that."

"Do you get to keep the land?"

"He says it's mine," she said. "I love it here."

"Is this land Norrid's to give?"

"If it isn't, he'll make it his," Loanda said easily. "What he wants, he gets."

He had wondered how she felt about Norrid. Now he knew. "I've been looking for someone I think is hiding out near here," he said, changing the subject. "I looked in all the caves in the bluffs at this end of the creek. Do you know of any others?"

"There are two big ones down close to Monotony," Loanda said. "I can't imagine anyone living in a cave, though."

258

"Not much different from a dugout."

"I wouldn't like that either."

She took up the potatoes and meat she had fried and set them on the table. Paxton turned his full attention to the food, almost forgetting his eagerness to look in that one cave near town that he hadn't explored. It seemed like a good bet that Gary Wirth would be there if he was still alive. Someone, probably Yount, had been close enough to see him go into that other cave early this morning.

As soon as he had worked his way through the stack of potatoes and meat, he got up, thanked Loanda for the supper and for keeping the Circle N hounds off his track, then started for the door.

"Are you going to walk down the creek?" she asked.

"I haven't seen my horse for quite awhile."

"Take Trinket. I won't need him."

She went with him to the corral and caught the horse and Paxton saddled him. As he rode away from the spring, he thought that his wound shortly after he arrived here had been the luckiest thing that could have happened to him. Loanda had taken a personal interest in keeping him alive, and she had managed to do it very well.

He stopped at Rooker's and found him home. His face broke into a grin when he saw his visitor.

"I saw them load your barrel, but I didn't figure they'd get you," he said. "There's something about a ghost that is hard to kill. Going back to look for your brother?"

Paxton nodded. "I have a feeling he's in that cave close to town if he's still alive. I stopped to ask if you think we could scare Norrid bad enough to make him tell us what he knows."

The grin left Rooker's face. "I don't know. Norrid's a tough nut. But he is becoming a believer in ghosts, I think. Bertha is making quite an impression on him with her predictions. What do you think he knows?"

"About everything there is to know about this country," Paxton said. "Loanda just told me he practically runs everything."

"You didn't have to ask Loanda that. I could have told you. Think he knows about the buried money?"

"I'm sure of it, but I'd like to know just how much he knows about it. I want to know about Kucek too."

"I'll sound him out about ghosts and

spirits the next time I see him," Rooker said. "If he's as jumpy as a scalded toad, it just might be that we can scare the truth out of him. Want me to help you look for your brother?"

Paxton shook his head. "No sense in risking your life too. It's not your brother I'm looking for."

"Maybe you'll do better alone anyway," Rooker said. "So far, nobody has been able to kill the ghost."

"They just haven't shot straight enough," Paxton said. "I'll see you after I find out what's in that cave."

He rode the horse slowly down the valley, making sure he didn't run into the Circle N coming back from their fruitless chase of the ghost that killed Al Zamora.

Approaching the bluff just above the cottonwood grove, he reined into its deep shadow, searching the bluff for the cave. He almost missed it. It was less than a hundred yards from the one he'd been exploring this morning when he'd been shot at.

Leaving the horse ground hitched, he moved quietly up to the cave. Pausing there, he listened intently. There was no sound. It wasn't likely that Yount would be here, he reasoned, even if Gary was. Yount was likely in town.

He moved inside, listened again, then pressed himself against the wall and called softly for Gary. The sound seemed amazingly loud after the dead silence he had been encountering.

From far back in the cave came an eager reply. Paxton's hopes leaped. But the next second they were dashed. Gary had called from far back in the cave. There was a sudden scramble nearby. That meant that someone else was in this cave too. That would have to be Caleb Yount. He was familiar with the cave; Paxton wasn't. Yount had him now where he'd been trying to get him all day, trapped at a decided disadvantage.

Chapter 23

Paxton slipped silently away from the spot where he had called. Yount would move toward that place. He waited, knowing that the advantage was all with Yount. He would know every nook in this cave. Paxton knew only the way out. But if he went that way, he'd be silhouetted against the night sky, a perfect target for anyone inside the cave.

Suddenly the interior of the cave exploded with the roar of a gun. The bullet had gone close to where Paxton had been. Paxton fired instantly at the flash of the gun. Then he dived to one side. It was barely fast enough. Yount's return shot chipped the rock inches from Paxton's head.

Paxton knew he had to get out of the cave. He couldn't hope to survive in here where Yount would likely find a protruding rock for protection while shooting at Paxton who would be in the open.

Retreating slowly toward the mouth of the cave, he stopped short of silhouetting himself. He could hear someone back in the cave moving quietly toward him. He reasoned that Yount must be almost to the spot where he had been when he called to Gary.

Yount fired again, missing Paxton by several feet. Paxton's return shot spanged off the cave wall and brought a laugh from Yount. He'd had some kind of protection.

Paxton hit the cave floor and rolled across as Yount fired at the spot where he'd been. Then before Yount would have time to think about Paxton's next move, Paxton dived through the mouth of the cave.

Yount fired swiftly, obviously taken by surprise by the sudden move. The first bullet missed completely; the second one just nicked Paxton's sleeve. Paxton hit the ground outside and rolled again, coming up against a small chokecherry bush. Diving around it, he aimed his gun at the cave's mouth. He had made it outside. Now the odds would be nearly even.

He waited in vain. Yount did not come out. Paxton thought about Gary in there, a prisoner of Yount. Yount hadn't killed him yet. But what would he do now that Paxton had located the place where he was holding him? As if to verify Paxton's worry,

Yount yelled from inside the cave.

"If you want your brother, you're going to have to come in and get him."

"Are you too big a coward to come out and face a man who knows what a gun is for?" Paxton challenged.

Yount laughed. "I don't have to come out. But you have to come in if you want to see your brother alive."

Paxton considered his next move. He certainly wasn't going to charge back into that cave. He'd never get to his brother, and Yount knew it. The moon, coming up later every night, hadn't appeared yet. If he was going to do anything, it would have to be before that moon lit up the outside of the cave.

He shifted his position to get away from a rock that was gouging him. His hand gripped the rock. It wasn't too big to throw. He heaved it at the far side of the cave mouth.

Yount immediately fired at the spot where it lit. Paxton left his chokecherry bush and dived toward the wall beside the mouth of the cave. As long as he stayed out in front, Yount might decide to spray the area with bullets.

He was halfway to the wall when Yount swung his fire toward him. Paxton was moving rapidly out of Yount's vision, but

Yount kept shooting and following Paxton's flight.

When Paxton finally reached the wall and wheeled his back against it, he realized that Yount was still trying to pick him off. He had come out of the cave. Paxton brought up his gun and fired at the flash of Yount's gun. He could vaguely make out his bulky figure.

Confidence surged up in Paxton as he realized he was now on even terms with Yount. Yount had apparently gambled that he could hit Paxton while he was scrambling for a safer hiding place than the chokecherry bush. He had lost.

After Paxton's first shot, Yount disappeared. Paxton waited for him to show himself but he heard and saw nothing. He was probably reloading his gun, Paxton guessed. Finally he moved away from the wall a few feet. Yount fired immediately from a gully on the far side of the cave mouth.

Paxton ducked back but then wormed his way across the cave opening where he could see the gully that he hadn't noticed before. Yount fired again when Paxton moved closer, but he was now some distance up the gully. Paxton followed, realizing that Yount was on the retreat. He had lost his gamble, and now he had no stomach for an even fight with Paxton.

Paxton reached the gully and moved forward as quietly as possible. When he didn't see or hear Yount, he stopped. Yount opened up then from a short distance ahead where he'd been waiting for Paxton to come closer. Paxton dived into the brush in the gully and waited until he got a good shot. Then he fired.

He realized he had missed, but Yount went scrambling on up the gully. Paxton followed for a few yards, then stopped. Yount was really on the run. Now was the time to get back to the cave and find Gary before Yount circled back there. Yount would kill Gary if he got to him again.

Paxton retreated down the gully to the cave and went inside. Back a short distance from the mouth, he stopped and called. Gary answered immediately. Guided by the sound of his voice, Paxton stumbled over the uneven floor of the cave until he found Gary bound against a big rock.

Kneeling, Paxton quickly cut the ropes. Striking a match, Paxton got his first look at his brother in over twenty years.

"I didn't think I'd ever get out of here alive," Gary said.

"We're not out yet. Let's get moving before he comes back."

"You didn't kill him?"

"He slipped up a gully and got away. Killing him isn't as important as getting you out of here."

"I won't argue with that," Gary said. "Do you think he'll come back?"

"He's sure to. He can't inherit that land till he kills one of us or scares us off."

"Your Uncle Joshua put us in a bad spot with the terms of his will."

"Doubt if he thought of it that way," Paxton said. "I guess I talked too much about wanting to see you. He figured this was a way to get us back together again."

Paxton started toward the mouth of the cave with Gary in tow. He wished he had an extra gun for his brother.

"Do you know your way around this cave?" he asked.

"No. Yount just brought me in here and tied me up. Kept telling me he'd bring you in, too, then he'd blow up the cave."

"Can you use a gun?"

"I can," Gary said, "but I'm not good with one."

Because he was thinking that Yount would have to try to kill them, he wasn't so surprised when he saw a gun flash ahead of them. A bullet ricocheted off the chalk rock close beside them.

Without aiming, Paxton fired at the flash. There was a yelp and then some scrambling.

"Come on," Paxton whispered. "Let's get him."

He ran toward the sound. That yelp had told him that Yount was hit. He wasn't hurt bad, judging from the way he was scrambling around.

Paxton followed the sound until he realized he was going away from the mouth of the cave. Yount had turned down a side tunnel that Paxton hadn't realized was there. He stopped.

"If we follow him in there, we'll be killed," he said softly to Gary. "All we really want is out of here. Let's go."

He ran toward the mouth of the cave, stumbling over the rocks and uneven floor. The late moon was up when they got outside.

"Where to now?" Gary asked.

"Let's go to Rooker's," Paxton said. "He's been my best friend since I got here. We'll try to find the lawyer tomorrow."

"Does this Rooker have anything to eat?" Gary asked.

"Didn't Yount feed you anything?"

"Just enough to keep my alive. I had the feeling he intended to kill me anyway."

"He's gone too far to leave any of us alive now," Paxton said. "He must have had some idea of using you as bait to catch me. Otherwise, he'd probably have killed you already."

Paxton reached Loanda's horse and put Gary up behind the saddle. Paxton didn't expect any more trouble from Yount tonight.

Rooker got out of bed at Paxton's knock and let them in. By the light of Rooker's lamp, Paxton saw that Gary looked something like he had expected him to. He should never have been fooled by Yount's lie that he was Gary Wirth.

The two brothers had a lot of years to cover, and they did it quickly while Rooker got some supper cooked for Gary. Paxton found out that Gary had received his letter from Mark Horn before Paxton had received his, so Gary had arrived at Monotony before Paxton did. He had found Horn just a couple of days after he arrived and had talked to him before Caleb Yount showed up. He'd been in hiding most of the time since then until Yount captured him.

"I haven't seen the spring," Gary admitted. "It had better be a good piece of land, considering what it has cost us already."

"It is," Paxton said, thinking of Loanda and her claim to it.

"That Tidrow girl is going to be a mite unhappy when you kick her off," Rooker said as he scooped potatoes and meat from the skillet to a plate.

"Somebody living on the place?" Gary asked.

Paxton nodded, sorting out his mixed emotions. He liked the spring, but he didn't like the idea of throwing Loanda off. She liked it too, and he really did owe her more than he could repay.

"Sam Tidrow's daughter claims it," Rooker said. "You rode up here on her horse."

Gary looked sharply at Paxton. "Did she loan it to you?"

Paxton nodded. "I was afoot. She saved my life twice. Taking her place away from her isn't going to be very good pay for what she's done."

Gary whistled softly. "Maybe you don't want to claim the land."

"It's not Loanda who owns the land now," Paxton said. "It's Elias Norrid. He says Loanda can have it, but I doubt if he'd let her own it. I'd like nothing better than to take that land away from Norrid."

While Gary ate hungrily, Paxton thought about Yount. What would he do now? He wasn't hurt much, he was sure. He apparently would go to any length to get that land. He'd probably guess that Paxton would bring Gary up the valley tonight and would go back into town tomorrow morning to find the lawyer. Yount would be waiting for them somewhere along the way.

At dawn, they were getting their horses ready. Rooker had found the black and brought him home. They still had Loanda's horse, so each one had a horse for the ride into town.

Paxton led the way across the creek and up on the ridge above the valley before turning toward town.

"Think he might be waiting for us on the valley road?" Rooker asked.

"Good chance of it. No point in risking it."

They stayed on the prairie until they came to town. Then Paxton reined down the slope to the second bench above the creek where the residences sat above the business district.

"Better leave our horses here," Paxton

suggested when they came to the edge of town. "No use in pointing out to everyone where Horn is staying."

They dismounted, ground hitched the horses, then walked to Mrs. Fenton's house. Paxton knocked and Mrs. Fenton jerked the door open. The way she moved told Paxton that things were not right.

"What happened?" he demanded.

Mrs. Fenton was almost hysterical. "A great big man broke in here just before dawn. He shoved me around and tore through the house till he found Mr. Horn. Then he grabbed him and dragged him out."

"Yount!" Paxton exclaimed. "Where did he take Horn?"

"I don't know," she wailed. "He threatened to kill me if I called for help."

"What if he kills Horn?" Gary asked.

Paxton shook his head. "Maybe he won't. Yount may use him for bait to catch us. If we go looking for Horn, Yount will ambush us."

"We've got to find him," Gary said.

"You're right," Paxton agreed, "and Yount knows it."

Chapter 24

Aggravation boiled through Paxton. He had thought he had Yount licked. Instead, he was really no closer to victory than he was before he found Gary.

"Maybe it's time to put the ghost to work again," Rooker said, rubbing his chin thoughtfully.

"A ghost isn't going to bring Horn back," Gary said.

Paxton watched Jeff Rooker closely. He not only liked the little man, he had developed a robust respect for him. Rooker loved practical jokes, but he had turned that fertile imagination into a valuable asset in Paxton's battle against the ones trying to kill him.

"What scheme have you got bubbling now?" Paxton asked.

"Don't know that there is one, but there might be. It's just possible that Norrid knows where Yount would take Horn. You asked last night if we could scare him into telling what he knows. Maybe we can."

"He won't know anything about Yount, will he?" Gary asked.

"Loanda says he runs this whole country and knows almost everything that is going on," Paxton said.

"It might be worth a try," Rooker said. "Let me go over and see Norrid. I'll find out how jumpy he is. You stay here and keep thinking where Yount might have taken Horn and how we can get him back without getting ourselves killed."

"That won't be easy," Paxton said.

"Suppose he took him to the cave where I was?" Gary asked when Rooker was gone.

"It's possible," Paxton said. "I doubt if he did though. He'd know that would be one of the first places we'd look."

"Maybe he wants us to find him."

"That's logical too," Paxton agreed. "Killing Horn wouldn't change that will. Killing one of us would."

Rooker was back in a few minutes. It was only a block and a half down the street from Mrs. Fenton's to Elias Norrid's big house.

"He is as nervous as a lamb in a coyote den," Rooker reported. "Would hardly talk to me. Blames me for some of his troubles at the spring. I talked to Bertha though.

She's planning another seance out at Sutcliffe's."

"When?" Paxton asked.

"Tonight." Rooker's black eyes were sparkling. "That gives us the chance we want."

"I hope we're not going to another seance," Paxton moaned.

Rooker shook his head. "Norrid isn't going either. That means he'll be home alone tonight. He's mighty jumpy about those spirits Bertha calls up. Why not have one of them show up outside Norrid's window? No telling what he might tell if he gets scared enough."

Paxton nodded. "That sounds like fun. Got an idea how to do it?"

"I'll get one," Rooker said. "You and Gary better stay right here today. Mrs. Fenton needs company, and you know Yount will be watching for you."

Paxton didn't like the inactivity. He had never won a battle yet by hiding. All Paxton asked was an even break with Yount, but that would be the one thing that Yount would make sure he didn't get.

Rooker rode out of town, and Paxton stationed himself close to a front window. He couldn't see much of the town from there and what he could see looked almost as dead as a ghost town.

In midafternoon, he saw a buggy come by from the direction of Norrid's. Bertha Norrid was driving alone. She would be heading for Sutcliffe's place to get ready for the seance tonight. Elias Norrid hadn't gone along. It was working out just as Rooker had said it would.

Jeff Rooker came back shortly after that, riding in from the west instead of coming in on the usual road. Paxton met him behind the house. He had a load of things in a big sack behind the saddle.

"Saw Bertha heading for Sutcliffe's," he said. "Half the town will be out there tonight, maybe most of it. Norrid will be mighty lonesome till we get there."

"What did you bring?" Paxton asked.

Rooker took the sack off the saddle and carried it into the house. "Just the things I figure we'll need," he said. He opened the sack. "First, here is your white coat and your white hat."

"I wouldn't have been surprised to see my white horse," Paxton said.

"Couldn't figure a way to use it on Norrid," Rooker said, ignoring Paxton's sarcasm. He dumped the sack. "Got some rope and some sacks. I figure we can make do with this."

Before sundown, it looked to Paxton like the town was experiencing a general exodus. Buggies and surreys and several riders headed up the creek. Sutcliffe was going to have a lot of company tonight.

Paxton waited impatiently for dark. Rooker hadn't revealed the details of his plan. Paxton doubted if he knew just what he was going to do until he got to Norrid's and saw how things were.

When Rooker gave the sign, Paxton picked up the big sack containing the rope, empty sacks, and his white hat and coat and followed Rooker out the back door. Gary was just a step behind him.

At Norrid's barn, they stopped. Rooker was grinning like a boy on a Halloween spree. "It's about the way I remembered it," he said softly. "I'm going to take this long rope and climb the windmill tower. One of you climb that big cottonwood next to it. I'll tie one end of the rope to the tower and throw the other end to you. Tie it to a limb as near the same height as you can."

Paxton didn't question the move but climbed the tree and tied the rope when Rooker threw it to him. He could see Elias Norrid reading by a lamp at the living room window.

Back at the barn, Rooker took the empty sacks and stuffed them with hay, using string to tie them so the finished product looked something like a man with head, arms and legs. Tying another rope around the dummy's neck, Rooker carried it out to the windmill. There, he threw the loose end of the rope over the rope stretched between the mill and the tree.

Pulling on the end of the rope, he dragged the limp dummy into the air.

"Get your ghost outfit on," Rooker whispered to Paxton. "Gary, can you groan like a ghost?"

Gary grinned. "Don't know how a ghost is supposed to groan, but I can sound like I'm dying."

"Close enough," Rooker said. "Get under Norrid's window and start when Dave is ready. I'll hang the dummy. There's enough light for Norrid to see it against the sky. It will be up to you, Dave, to make him talk."

Paxton nodded and slipped into his white coat and hat. Moving around to the back door of the house, he silently stepped inside. He couldn't see what Rooker was doing, but he knew without looking. He had barely gotten in the house when he heard a low moan that grew to a horrible groan. Moving around to a spot where he could see through a partition doorway, he watched the reaction of Norrid.

The book dropped from Norrid's hands, and he jerked his head around at the open window. The groan came again and Norrid upset the chair getting back from the window. Then Paxton heard a new moan from farther away. That would be Rooker making sure that Norrid saw the dummy swinging fifteen feet above the earth.

By crouching, Paxton could barely see the dummy through the window. The ropes holding it up were invisible in the darkness but the dummy stood out, swaying gently in the breeze.

"I'm coming for you, Elias," Gary moaned from under the window.

Norrid dived for his gun belt lying on a chair, falling over a footstool he'd been using. Getting up, he lunged again for his gun and wheeled back to the window. Poking the gun out the window, he fired twice at the dummy. Paxton could see from the way the dummy jerked and swung that he had hit it. Rooker pulled it a little higher.

"You can't kill a ghost," Gary moaned under the window.

Norrid squalled like a terrified baby and

fired twice more at the dummy. Gary's moan turned to an eerie laugh. "Bullets can't hurt me, Elias. I'm coming for you tonight."

Norrid screamed and fired again. Then the hammer fell on an empty chamber. Now that Norrid's gun was empty, Paxton knew it was his time to move. He stepped into the room.

"Over here, Elias," he said in a high pitched voice.

Norrid wheeled, his eyes bugging out of his face when he saw Paxton. He jerked up his gun and squeezed the trigger three times. Only clicks rewarded him. Norrid glared at the gun, sobbing like a heart-broken child. Then he threw the gun at Paxton who only had to duck to let it sail past him. Norrid crumpled down in the corner, sobbing hysterically.

"Why did you kill the Greers?" Paxton asked.

"I didn't! I didn't!" Norrid wailed.

Gary, just outside the open window, began moaning again. "I'm coming for you, Elias, unless you tell the truth."

Norrid's nerves were beyond repair. "All right," he wailed. "I hired Kucek to do it."

"Why?" Paxton shot at him. "Was it the spring?"

"Yes," Norrid moaned. "Water for my cows. The money buried there."

"What do you know about the money?"

"Can't find it," Norrid said. "I found out today that Kucek was in the gang who hid the money there. He wants it." He sobbed louder. "Now I'll never get it."

Paxton hid his shock. No wonder Kucek was willing to kill the Greers. He was after the money the same as Joshua.

"Does Loanda get the land at the spring?"

"I — I'll give it to her if you'll just go away," Norrid said, lifting terrified eyes to Paxton.

"Why are you trying to kill Paxton?"

"He came here to get revenge for Roy Greer's death. He may be after me."

"If you live, will you let him alone?"

"Anything, anything," Norrid agreed eagerly. Gary picked up his moaning singsong at the window. "I'll come back and get you the minute you break your promise."

"I'll keep my promise," Norrid wailed.

"Where is Caleb Yount?" Paxton asked.

"Don't know," Norrid whimpered. "He was to help me, but he ran off with the lawyer. Don't know where he went."

"Don't lie," Gary threatened from beneath the window.

"I ain't lying," Norrid sobbed. "What else can I do?"

"Go to Sutcliffe's and warn them not to cause Paxton any more trouble," Paxton said. He had to get Norrid away before he discovered their hoax.

"I'll do it," Norrid promised. "First thing in the morning."

"Now!" Paxton snapped.

Gary moaned louder than ever and Norrid stared at the window. Rooker added to the moans and let the dummy fall to the ground with a soft crunch. Norrid leaped up and charged for the back door and out to the barn, sobbing like a baby.

In a minute, Norrid's horse burst out of the barn with Norrid clinging to him. He charged at a gallop up the street, turning into the river road. Rooker came from the mill, doubled over with laughter.

"The angel, Gabriel, couldn't have scared him more."

"He's headed for Sutcliffe's, all right," Paxton agreed. "We found out a lot of things but not where Yount is holding Horn."

"Let's get this stuff out of here before he comes back," Gary said.

It took only a few minutes to get the rope untied from the windmill tower and the tree. They emptied the sacks and gathered up the ropes and the sacks and headed back to Mrs. Fenton's.

"You got his promise not to bother you any more," Rooker said. "Let's make sure he keeps that promise."

"How will we do that?"

"You show up on your white horse at Sutcliffe's. That should be the clincher."

Paxton nodded. He'd gone this far; he might as well follow through. Getting their horses, they rode hard up the creek to the sod barn. There, Paxton switched to the white horse, and they turned across the creek toward Sutcliffe's less than a mile away.

Two hundred yards short of Sutcliffe's house, they stopped. Only soft candlelight came from the windows of the house, but a couple of bonfires in the yard lighted the scene outside. People were in bunches around the yard. Rooker rode on alone. He was back in a minute.

"Norrid's horse is there, lathered like he'd been run through a soap factory. Take the ridge along this side and circle back of Sutcliffe's house," he said to Paxton.

Paxton nodded and reined the white horse toward the ridge, taking his time. Rooker and Gary would need to get in position to sound the alarm. When he broke out on the ridge, silhouetted from the house and yard below, a wild yell and an eerie moan wafted up from below.

Paxton put the white horse to a slow lope. At first there was a solitary scream down below and then bedlam broke loose. Screams and yells came from every section of the yard. There was a wild scramble for horses and buggies and more than one collision occurred before all the horses and buggies were strung out on the road toward town. Within minutes the place was quiet although the candles and the bonfires were still burning.

Paxton put his horse off the ridge and sent him flying down the valley toward the creek and across to the sod barn. He found Rooker and Gary already there.

"Ain't nobody going to doubt you're a ghost now," Rooker shouted gleefully. "I heard one man say, 'He's here already,' so Norrid had delivered his message."

"What now?" Gary asked.

"Dave will get rid of that white outfit and hide his horse, and we'll all go down to my place for a good night's sleep and funny dreams." He laughed again.

They had barely gotten the horses taken care of and settled inside Rooker's dugout when a shout came from the creek bottom in front of the house.

"Send the ghost out. Let's see him scare the gun out of my hands."

"Kucek!" Rooker exclaimed. "That's the voice of the man who killed Roy."

"Looks like I'm finally going to meet him," Paxton said. "I came all this way to get him."

"This ain't no time to face Kucek," Rooker objected. "You can bet he ain't alone. He's probably got Ortis with him and no telling who else."

"Maybe that deputy, Tug Buskey, is with him," Gary said.

"I doubt that," Rooker said. "After Buskey and his posse got spooked by the ghost, he ain't liable to want any more of it, even if he's figured out the ghost is staying with me."

Paxton knew that this probably wasn't the time and place to face Kucek. But he'd come too far and waited too long to let this opportunity slip away.

Chapter 25

"You can't see him out there," Rooker said. "He'll have the advantage even if he is alone."

Paxton saw the wisdom of that, but he had never backed off from a challenge. He didn't like the idea now, although he had survived by subscribing to the idea that it wasn't wise to let the enemy pick the time and the place for a battle.

A gun boomed and a bullet splintered a board in the door of the dugout. "Is the ghost a coward as well as a fake?" Kucek yelled.

Paxton started for the door, but Gary grabbed his arm. "You'll never get through the door."

Paxton stopped. "Who's with you out there?" he yelled.

"Who says anybody is?" Kucek yelled back.

"Only cowards bring helpers along," Paxton shouted.

"Who are you calling a coward?" Kucek

screamed. "Do I have to come in there and drag you out?"

"You're welcome to try," Paxton shouted back.

"He won't do that," Rooker said confidently.

"I'll meet you on the street of Monotony tomorrow morning at nine," Kucek shouted. "I'll be alone. You'd better be too."

"I'll be there," Paxton yelled back. "I want to see you when we meet." He was letting Kucek pick the time and place, but this was a decision he could accept.

Two more bullets thudded into the dugout door followed by the sound of galloping horses.

"There was more than one," Rooker said. "I figured as much."

"Are you really going to face him tomorrow?" Gary asked fearfully.

"Of course," Paxton said. "This may be my only chance to get the man who killed Roy. Besides, he has challenged me. I can't back out."

"We'll all go in early tomorrow," Rooker said. "We'll make sure Kucek doesn't have anyone hidden somewhere to do his shooting for him."

"You'll have to watch out for Yount too," Gary warned.

"I know that," Paxton said. "I think Kucek will be alone tomorrow. He's a gunman. A gunfighter is proud of his ability to beat any other gunfighter. Tonight was a trap; pride didn't count. Tomorrow will be different."

"Nothing is below the dignity of Yount," Gary said. "If he finds out about the fight, he'll ambush you before Kucek gets a chance."

Paxton shook his head. "Not till after the fight. Why should he risk a gun battle if Kucek will take care of his problem for him? I won't have to worry about Yount until after I beat Kucek, if I do."

"Kucek is a good gunfighter," Rooker said. "But he's going up against the ghost of a gunfighter this time."

"That ghost business won't cut any ice with Kucek."

"Probably not," Rooker admitted. "He wouldn't have come here tonight to challenge you if he believed the ghost story."

"There's still Ortis to consider too," Paxton said. "Norrid wants me dead, and Ortis is his man."

"If you beat Kucek, Ortis won't want any part of you," Rooker said.

The three were mounted ready to ride shortly after dawn the next morning. No one had been too interested in breakfast so it had been a short meal. Paxton agreed it would be just as well to wait in town as out here. And there was the chance that they might get on the trail of Yount and Horn.

"Do you know what day this is?" Gary asked as they rode down the valley. "If I haven't missed my calculations, this is October 3. Tomorrow is the last day we can claim Joshua's land."

"We'll look for Horn as soon as I deal with Kucek," Paxton said.

"I hope so," Gary said.

Paxton knew that had slipped out before he thought how it sounded. There was doubt in Gary's mind that Paxton could beat Kucek. Doubt was a word a gunfighter never used.

"Better split up here," Rooker said when they were within a couple of miles of town. "I'll ride straight up the road into town. Everybody knows me."

Paxton nodded. "I'll swing left. Gary can go right. Meet you at the church."

"We can watch the town from there," Rooker said.

Paxton went up the slope to the left while Gary crossed the creek to the right. Paxton listened for any sound along the river road. Even if there was an ambush set up there, the killer should recognize that Rooker wasn't Paxton or Gary. Rooker was depending on that.

There was no sound and Paxton found Rooker at the church when he got there.

"Town's popping," Rooker said excitedly when he saw Paxton. "They know about the fight at nine but that ain't what's got them fired up."

"What happened?"

"A rider came in from Ogallala. They've got one of those telegraphs up there, you know. He says they got a message that Dull Knife and his Cheyennes have broken out of their reservation down in Oklahoma."

Paxton nodded. "I'm not surprised. Dull Knife and Little Wolf were threatening to break out when I was there. The way the soldiers were guarding them, it looked impossible, but I'm not surprised they made it."

"They think they're coming this way," Rooker said.

"Do they know where they are now?"

"The man said they crossed the Kansas Pacific Railroad a ways east of Fort Wallace, and they think they're heading for their old hunting grounds in the Dakotas or Montana or maybe Canada where some of their brothers are already sitting, laughing at the soldiers."

Paxton nodded. "They could come right through here."

"They wouldn't send a man all the way down from Ogallala to warn us if they didn't think so."

Gary rode in then, and Rooker repeated what he had told Paxton. Gary frowned at the news.

"How many of them are there?"

"Thousands, the man said."

"I doubt that," Paxton said. "There aren't nearly that many in Dull Knife's outfit. And a lot of them are squaws and children."

"The army can take care of that many," Gary said confidently.

"Then why haven't they?" Rooker demanded. "They could be in southwestern Nebraska right now, and the army hasn't stopped them yet."

"I think Kucek is more of a threat to us than the Indians," Gary said.

"It's a long time till nine," Paxton said. "Jeff, you keep an eye out for anybody taking squatters rights at a window or doorway along the street. I'm going to do some inquiring about Yount."

"You be careful or you won't even be

around for the nine o'clock battle," Rooker said.

Paxton headed up the street with Gary at his side. His eyes darted into every corner and alley as he passed, but the town was centered around the messenger from Ogallala. He was still explaining his news to men as they came running up to ask about it. He was on the porch of the bank. Norrid probably hadn't had that many people in front of his bank since it opened.

Paxton and Gary stayed on the opposite side of the street until they were past the bank. Then Paxton cut across the street to the general store. If anybody would know about Yount, it would be Upshaw. Getting him to tell what he knew would be the problem.

They stepped into the store. Upshaw saw them and backed toward the rear door.

"Hold it," Paxton yelled. "I want to ask you something."

"I ain't talking to no ghost," Upshaw said, and he sprinted, as fast as a man his size could, toward the back door.

"We're wasting our time," Paxton said.

A man Paxton didn't know was coming into the store as they turned to go out. Gary touched his arm.

"Have you seen the lawyer, Mark Horn?"

The man shrugged and shook his head. "Not for a long time."

"How about Caleb Yount?"

"The fat man? Yeah, I saw him just this morning, but I don't know where he is now."

"That's as good as we're going to do," Paxton said, leading Gary out of the store. "Yount is still in town. So if Horn is alive, he has to be somewhere in or near town."

They went back to the church, again avoiding the crowd in front of the bank. Rooker met them, his eyes still on the upper end of the street.

"He hasn't showed up yet," he said. "Even if he is alone, I wouldn't trust him not to try some trick."

"I'll watch for one," Paxton said.

"So will we," Rooker said. "Gary, you go to the hotel and climb up to the roof. Find a spot where you can see if there are any extra gun hands slipping into town. I'll watch from the church belfry."

"Don't either one of you get into the fight," Paxton warned.

"It's your fight," Rooker agreed. "Kucek might come alone, or he might bring half the Circle N with him."

"I doubt that," Paxton said. "He's too proud to ask for help that people could see."

Paxton waited in front of the church while Gary disappeared into the hotel and Rooker started up the ladder into the church belfry. There had never been enough money to buy a bell but the place for it had been built when the church was erected.

Paxton watched the road leading into the main street. Kucek would come down that unless he was going to try some trick. He saw a dozen riders go up the street and fan out in different directions to the south and west on the prairie. They were going to check on the Indian scare, he supposed.

When they were gone, the town turned its attention to the big news before the Indian scare, the gunfight between Kucek and the ghost. People had been exposed to Kucek's speed with a gun, so there would be few bets placed on Paxton.

Rooker called down from the belfry. "Kucek is coming down the road. He's alone."

Paxton nodded and checked his gun. Would Kucek come in shooting, or would he stall and try to break Paxton's nerves?

Kucek appeared at the far end of the street and rode directly to the pool hall as if that was his destination. Dismounting, he went inside. Paxton continued to wait.

He wouldn't let it shatter his nerves.

In a few minutes, Paxton saw Icky coming down the side of the hotel. He should have been at the pool hall cleaning. Icky came directly across the street from the hotel.

"I got a message for you," Icky said nervously.

"From Kucek?"

Icky nodded. "He's waiting at the pool hall."

"If he expects me to come there, he'll have a long wait. He said he'd meet me on the street."

"That still may be what he intends to do," Icky said. "He said to tell you if I could find you, that he has killed two Greers, and now he is ready to kill one of their relatives."

"Tell him I'll be ready whenever he is," Paxton said. "But he won't be shooting at an old man with his back turned this time."

Paxton watched Icky run back across the street and turn down the alley behind the hotel. He felt the cold lump growing in his stomach. It wouldn't be long now.

Chapter 26

"Icky make it to the pool hall yet?" Paxton asked Rooker above him.

"Yeah," Rooker said. "At least I think so. I can't see the back of the buildings over there."

"We should be seeing Kucek before long."

The street was as empty now as it had been full when he had first arrived and the messenger from Ogallala was here. Sweeping the front of the buildings along the street, Paxton could see faces at the windows and open doors, waiting expectantly.

Suddenly, Paxton's attention was pulled to Gary on top of the hotel. He was jabbing a finger toward the alley behind the business places.

"Coming down the alley?" Paxton asked softly.

Gary nodded. Paxton waved and moved out into the street. Kucek apparently planned to surprise him. If he could get as close as the corner of the hotel, for instance, before showing himself, Paxton, if unwarned, would have been startled for an instant. Just a split second advantage could mean the difference between two fast gunfighters.

As he moved along the street, he shot a glance up at Gary. He was pointing in the direction of the bank or Upshaw's store, Paxton couldn't tell which. Apparently, Kucek was behind one or the other of those two buildings now.

Kucek would still have the advantage of knowing at exactly what second he would step out into the street. But no matter what he did now, he wasn't going to surprise Paxton much.

Paxton had moved up almost to the corner of the hotel when Kucek suddenly burst into the street from the far corner of the bank. He must have had some warning that his trick had been discovered. He was still a hundred feet from Paxton, too far for an effective surprise.

As he came around the corner of the bank, he had his gun in his hand. At the first glimpse of Kucek, Paxton planted his feet, his hand darting to his gun. Kucek had outsmarted himself in one detail. He had his gun ready to fire before he had stopped his motion. His first shot, fired on the move, missed its target by inches.

Paxton was steady. The situation was not new to him, but it was always a bone-chilling experience. He squeezed off his first shot just as Kucek was bringing his gun in line for a second try.

Kucek was jolted backward as he fired. He sat down in the street with a thud and a puff of dust while Paxton stood his ground. That second shot of Kucek's had gone over Paxton's head by several feet.

Kucek tried to raise his gun for another try, but it sagged more and more and finally slid from his hand as he toppled to one side. Paxton had the chance now to get his first good look at the gunman. A chill ran through him. It was almost as if he were looking in a mirror. No wonder he'd been mistaken for Kucek. He held his gun steady for a moment longer, then slowly put it back in the holster and turned back to the church.

People appeared on porch steps and stared first at Kucek then at Paxton. Kucek's reputation here was well known. Paxton had not drawn his gun in Monotony before. He saw the men on the porch of the hotel as he walked back down the street. Awe was plain on their faces.

Rooker was out of the belfry by the time Paxton reached the church. "You couldn't get a nickel bet against a dollar anywhere in town now that you're real flesh and blood," he said gleefully. "Everybody thought there wasn't a faster gun west of the Missouri than Kucek. He's dead, and you ain't even got a scratch."

"He may have been faster," Paxton said, feeling the sickness start to well up in him as it did after every such encounter. "He just outsmarted himself. He wasn't set when he fired that first shot."

"No matter what happened, it's the end result that counts. He's dead, and you're not."

Gary came across the street and a couple of men followed him. They stared at Paxton.

"Ain't you even hit?" one asked softly.

Paxton shrugged. "Not a scratch."

Icky came running across from the hotel. "I told them!" he shouted, "I told everybody! They can't kill a ghost!"

The two men backed off a few steps, then turned and hurried back to the hotel. Gary turned to Paxton, his face as pale as a sheet.

"Does that avenge the two Greers?" he asked.

Paxton sensed the reprimand in his voice. "It's all I can do," he said. "I can't bring Josh and Roy back to life, but the man who killed them is no longer running free and bragging about it."

"You did what you came here to do," Rooker said.

"I still have to find Mark Horn and get this estate settled," Paxton said.

Men were swarming into the street now and gathering around the spot at the corner of the bank where Kucek had fallen. No one was coming down to see Paxton. That suited Paxton; he wanted to get away. He'd heard lots of stories about gunfighters killing a man and laughing it off. It had never been that way with him.

"Let's look in those caves for Yount," he suggested.

Any activity would be better than staying here. While the town looked at the dead gunfighter and talked about the man who had killed him, Paxton and his brother and Rooker went down to the creek behind the church. Turning upstream through the grove of cottonwoods, they reached the bluffs where the two caves were. Gary shuddered as he looked at them.

"One of us had better stay outside and make sure no one slips up on us," Paxton said, remembering how he had almost been killed coming out of that empty cave the first time he'd been here.

"I'll do that," Rooker volunteered.

Paxton moved into the cave cautiously, remembering how he had found Yount in the other cave the other night. But everything was silent now.

"He probably took Horn to the other cave where he held me," Gary said softly.

"Could be," Paxton agreed. He called but got no answer. It didn't take long to check the length of the cave.

Back outside, they moved up the bluff to the other cave. Here, Paxton was even more cautious. But again they found the cave deserted.

Rooker shook his head when they came out. "Where could he be hiding him?"

"Probably right where we'd least expect him to be," Paxton said. "In town."

"Where could he hide a man in town?" Gary asked.

"How about where you hid?" Paxton said. "Who would look in Horn's own office for him?"

"Could be," Gary agreed. "I stayed there for several days, and nobody knew I was there except Icky. He knew but didn't tell."

"He knows about everything that goes

on in town," Rooker said. "He might know if Yount is holding Horn in his own office."

"We'll ask him if we see him," Paxton said. "If we don't, we'll assume Yount is there and act accordingly."

They went back down the creek, then turned up beside the church to the street. Paxton led the way across the street to the far corner of the hotel. There were still people in the street, but they paid no attention to the three moving over to the hotel.

Going the length of the hotel, Paxton turned along the back of the building. From there they got a good look at the rear of the lawyer's little office. It looked deserted, but it had looked deserted when Gary had used it for a hiding place too.

"Let's see if Icky is home," Paxton said.

They moved along the side of the hotel to the steps leading down to Icky's living quarters. They knocked but got no answer. Icky was probably enjoying every moment of the excitement created by the gunfight.

"This is my kind of work," Paxton said when they came back up the steps. "I'll see if there is anyone in that office."

Rooker and Gary stayed at the top of the steps while Paxton walked toward the street. When he was even with the lawyer's little office, he turned toward it. If Yount was inside, he wouldn't have much chance to see his approach.

Paxton was over halfway to the office when a gun roared. The bullet snapped past Paxton and thudded into the side of the hotel. Paxton automatically ducked and dived toward the side of the office where no one inside could see him.

Rooker snapped a shot at the office from the safety of the stairwell beside the hotel. Paxton bent low and went around the corner of the office building. Coming to the back door, he rose enough to get power in his legs and hit the door with all his strength.

The door burst open, and Paxton swept his gun over the interior. He saw Horn sitting tied at one end of the little back room. Then he saw Yount in the front part of the office.

Yount fired twice and missed both shots. He was too nervous and frightened to be accurate, Paxton realized as he tried to get a sight on the big man. Yount ducked out of sight behind the partition.

Paxton charged across the room. Just as he reached the doorway into the main office, he saw Yount launch himself at the big window in the front of the building. The front door was locked; the only way out was the window.

Glass shattered and sprayed over the board sidewalk as Yount went through the window. Paxton ran to the window. He was amazed at how fast a man of Yount's size could move. By the time he reached the window, Yount had ducked around the corner of the building. From there, he dashed across the porch of the bank. Paxton could barely see him from the front window.

Leaning past the jagged glass that still clung to the window frame, he fired a shot at Yount, but the angle was bad and he knew he had missed. Yount plunged across the porch to the hitchrack where three horses stood. He took the one farthest from the lawyer's office. Hidden from the office window, he mounted and, hanging low over the side of the horse, sent him up the side street beyond the bank.

Paxton, trying to find a piece of Yount big enough to make a target, gave up in frustration. He could have shot the horse, but Yount wasn't that important. Paxton's goal was to get Horn away from him. He had already accomplished that.

Running to the back door, he watched to see where Yount went. He saw him go straight west through the residential area on the second bench of land above the creek and continue on up the steep slope to the level of the prairie. He showed no sign of slowing down as he disappeared beyond the bluffs.

As Rooker and Gary came across from the hotel, Paxton turned to Horn and began untying the ropes binding his wrists and ankles.

"I need a drink," Horn croaked. "He hasn't given me any water since yesterday."

Paxton relayed the request to Rooker as he came in, and Rooker turned back to find some water. Gary came on in and crouched beside Paxton in front of the lawyer.

"Did he feed you?" Paxton asked.

Horn shook his head. "He didn't care whether I lived or died."

"Can you stand up?" Paxton asked.

"Haven't had a chance to try since he threw me in here."

"Why didn't you yell?" Gary asked.

"All he needed was an excuse to shoot me," Horn said. "I knew where I was. I heard people passing by. But if I'd chirped up, he'd have shot me and probably gotten away before anybody could have caught him."

Rooker arrived with a cup of water. Horn gulped it all down. He moved around the office with Paxton's help, stretching stiff muscles.

A yell sounded in the street and Paxton's attention was jerked away from the lawyer. There was the sound of a galloping horse being brought to a sliding halt in front of the bank.

"Something's wrong," Rooker yelled and dived out the back door.

Paxton was only a step behind Rooker. They ran down the alley between the lawyer's office and the bank. A man was sitting on his horse, waving his arms excitedly.

"Indians!" he yelled. "They're swarming over the prairie like fleas on a dog."

"Anybody killed?" one man asked.

"They've killed everybody they've seen, I think," the man said. "They're southwest of here, but they might come this way. We've got to get ready to fight."

Paxton thought of Loanda out at the spring. That spring must be right in the path of the Indians.

Chapter 27

Paxton forgot everything that had already happened today as his mind concentrated on Loanda alone at the spring. Rooker had suddenly lost interest in what was happening here in town too.

"My place!" he yelled. "They'll burn it."

"Can't burn much of a dugout," Paxton said. But he knew they could destroy everything in it. "I'm going to see if they hit the spring."

Paxton started on a run toward the church where he had left his horse when he'd ridden in this morning. Then he checked himself. Only fools and heroes destined to die went dashing off to the rescue without considering what they could do once they got there.

He thought of the Indians he had seen in Dull Knife's camp at Fort Reno. There were far too many of them for any band of homesteaders to stop. Only a well-organized regiment of cavalry could stop them. If they had struck at any of the places along the

Cottonwood, there wouldn't be much anybody could do about it now.

Then he remembered how Indians often broke up into small raiding parties, especially if the band was traveling fast. These foraging parties raided quickly and rushed back to the main band. A few extra guns could help turn away such a marauding band.

Gary ran from the lawyer's office, demanding to know where Paxton was going.

"Out to see what happened along the creek," Paxton said. "Find someone to take care of Horn then come on out. We'll meet you at the spring. You know where that is, don't you?"

Gary nodded. "I can find it. Think the Indians might have gotten the Tidrow girl?"

"Maybe," Paxton said, feeling the urgency driving him again. "I've got to find out."

Even as he turned away, it struck him that these Indians were not likely to carry off a woman. They were traveling fast because the army was after them. Captives would slow them down. They certainly wouldn't want any white women captives with them in case the army caught up with them. But they wouldn't hesitate to kill both men and women if they resisted their raids. Paxton couldn't imagine Loanda not putting up some resistance if they tried to steal her horses or burn her house.

When Paxton reached the church, Rooker was almost beside him. Their horses were still standing behind the church where they had left them when they arrived in town this morning for Paxton to face Kucek.

"Think we're too late?" Rooker asked as they mounted.

"Probably," Paxton said. "If that man saw the Indians riding through, they are probably well to the north by now. But we've got to find out what they did."

Paxton led the way out of town at a pace that matched the turmoil inside him. He wouldn't admit even to Rooker the worry and dread that drove him. A half mile from town, he swung up a gully that led toward the flat prairie above the creek.

"Too much danger of an ambush down there," he yelled at Rooker who was following. Rooker nodded.

They were southwest of town now and would be nearer Sutcliffe's than any other home if they continued in that direction. Passing the highest bluffs, Paxton put his horse on a direct route to the spring. Then as they were crossing the road leading from the creek up to Sutcliffe's, Paxton suddenly threw up his hand while bringing his horse to a stop. Rooker reined in beside him.

"Who's that?" Rooker gasped, staring at the bloody mutilated body at the side of the trail.

The clothes were torn off, scalp gone, fingers cut off, and slashes and cuts all over the body.

"Yount," Paxton said. "The size tells that. He came this way."

"Must have run right into them," Rooker said softly. "All they got from him was a horse."

"I wouldn't want that to happen to a mad dog," Paxton added in a subdued tone. "At least we know the Indians have passed this point."

"No danger of any stragglers?"

"Might be. Let's ride. We'll take care of Yount later."

"I want to see how Sutcliffe made out," Rooker said. "Looks like they were headed his way."

Paxton nodded. "I'll go on to the spring."

"Look," Rooker said quickly, pointing to the south. "Circle N riders."

"Maybe they're looking for Indians too," Paxton said.

"Or you and me," Rooker added. "You took care of Kucek and the Indians finished off Yount. But Norrid is set on getting rid of you. He's still got his gunfighter, Ortis."

"I'll cross that bridge when I get to it," Paxton said. "I'm going to see about Loanda."

"I'll come to the spring as soon as I see what happened to Sutcliffe," Rooker said, and he kicked his horse up the road.

Paxton nudged his horse into a gallop again. The Circle N riders didn't follow. It looked to him like the Indians must have come on a line almost even with the spring. They would fan out a ways on either side. They surely must have found Loanda's place. He hoped she had been gone when they hit.

From the top of the bluff, he could barely see Rooker's place across the creek. The door of the dugout appeared intact but the corral where Rooker kept his horses was torn down. A column of smoke rose from it where they had piled brush and set fire to it and probably anything they thought would be of value to the man who lived there. They'd hit here, all right. Rooker probably wouldn't have anything left in the house, but they'd been lucky that Paxton had had that appointment in town with Kucek this morning.

As he spurred his horse on toward the spring, he looked off to the north where the Indians had apparently gone. If they kept straight on they'd likely cross the Union Pacific somewhere close to Ogallala. He wondered if the soldiers were aware of that. There was no way to get word to them.

Breaking over the hill above the spring, he reined in. The house was still standing. Maybe the Indians hadn't struck here. There was nothing moving down there. Then he saw that the corral was open. Loanda kept at least two horses there all the time. Those were gone.

As he started down the slope, alert for signs of trouble, he saw a horse with his head drooping off to the right. That horse must surely belong to an Indian. It was obvious even from this distance that it had been ridden hard.

Paxton moved ahead cautiously. Nobody around here would ride a horse that hard. The Indians, however, fleeing ahead of the army, might ride a horse to death, then steal one to replace him.

When he got close enough, he saw that

the brand was a Diamond 7. There was no ranch near here that used that brand so far as Paxton knew. This horse had probably been stolen somewhere in Kansas.

He had his revolver in his hand and his finger on the trigger as he rode cautiously around the horse. If the Indian who had ridden that horse was hiding nearby, waiting to kill any man who came near to take his horse, he'd better find him now. If he went down to the house and an Indian was lurking out there, he'd be sure to sneak in and kill him.

A complete circle around the horse flushed nothing but a jackrabbit. There obviously was no Indian out here. He must have taken one of Loanda's horses. Angry at himself for being too cautious, he kicked his horse on toward the house.

He could feel sorry for the Indians. They had been rooted out of their homes and had died like flies in a strange land. But right now, he wasn't wasting any sympathy on them. If they had harmed Loanda in any way, he'd run them down and butcher them one by one.

He caught himself with a start. Maybe he was as savage as they were. But that thought was drowned in the realization of how much Loanda meant to him. He hadn't allowed himself to think of her as anything other than someone from the enemy camp who had saved his life. It came as a shock to him to realize that she had worked her way into his life deeply enough that concern for her overshadowed everything else when she was in danger.

He abandoned his cautious approach and rode directly up to the house. He still held his gun in his hand, but there was no stir anywhere. He hit the ground and moved up to the door which stood open. Leaping inside, he scanned the interior. The house was empty.

The two chairs were overturned and a bench was on its side in the middle of the floor. Clothes and papers were strung over the room. The Indians had made a rapid search for anything of value to them. There was no sign that they had tried to burn the house. They must have been in a big hurry.

Paxton looked around for any sign of a scuffle which would indicate that Loanda had been kidnapped. But amid all this destruction, a fight would have done less damage than had already been done.

Stepping back outside, he debated whether to go after the Indians on the chance that they had taken her along or to go to the Circle N and see if she was there.

He had decided earlier that the Indians wouldn't take any women prisoners because of the retaliation by the army when they were caught. The Indians probably had high hopes of escaping to Canada, but some of their leaders must be practical enough to know that their chances of reaching Canada were very slim. And besides, they wouldn't want to add to their troubles if they were captured.

If the Indians had taken Loanda, they'd either kill her or turn her loose soon. There probably wasn't much he could do if they had taken her, but he had to know and try to rescue her if she was a captive.

He had just started circling the yard, hoping to find something that would give him a clue whether or not Loanda was with the Indians, when Rooker rode over the knoll.

"Did you find Sutcliffe?" Paxton asked, reining up.

"He's all right," Rooker said. "He hid in the cellar while the Indians were tearing everything apart. His wife was in town. He's pretty well shaken up. Didn't sound much like a preacher when I left him."

Gary came up the creek valley with another rider slumped over his saddle.

"Ain't that the lawyer, Horn?" Rooker asked.

Paxton nodded. "Didn't think he was able to ride this far. Why did he come?"

Paxton and Rooker met Gary and the lawyer close to the house. Paxton was puzzled by Horn's presence, but he couldn't get Loanda out of his mind.

"Mr. Horn insisted on coming along to show me the way," Gary said. "I've never been to the spring before."

"I thought he was on his last legs," Rooker said bluntly.

"I had to see what they'd done to the spring," Horn said, the ride obviously having drained his strength. "Where's the Tidrow girl?"

"I don't know," Paxton said, the worry flooding over him again. "I was trying to find out if she had been taken by the Indians. She might be at the Circle N."

"More than likely the Circle N," Rooker said hopefully.

"You can read signs," Paxton said. "You scout to the north and see if you can find anything that says there was a white woman with the Indians. I'll check the Circle N."

"You watch your step down there," Rooker warned. "They still want your hide."

Paxton nodded. "Gary, you stay with

Mr. Horn. We'll be back as soon as we find out anything."

Paxton spurred his horse toward the Circle N. If Loanda wasn't there, the chances were that he'd never see her alive again.

He was about two miles from the spring when he caught a glimpse of horses ahead. He reined up and waited. If those were Indians, he'd have to make a run for it. But when they topped the next knoll, he saw that they were white riders. That had to be the Circle N. There weren't that many riders in any one outfit around here except the Circle N.

They seemed as surprised at seeing Paxton as he was at meeting them out there. They were close enough now that Paxton could recognize the white mane of Elias Norrid at the head. Sam Tidrow and Vic Ortis were beside him.

Norrid shouted something and Ortis pulled a rifle and took a shot at Paxton. Paxton wheeled his horse and headed back to the spring. Rooker had warned him that the Circle N would be after his hide. Apparently, Norrid was determined to kill him any way he could.

Paxton's horse was weary from the long run out from town, but now Paxton demanded the utmost from the old horse. He doubted if he would be able to keep ahead of the Circle N until he got back to the spring.

Chapter 28

As he rode, bending low over the saddle, Paxton kept looking back. He couldn't see Loanda among the riders. He'd hate to think she was among those trying to kill him, but if she was, at least he'd know the Indians didn't have her.

The old horse showed magnificent courage in his dash back to the house by the spring. In spite of running since he'd left town, he still managed to put out a real burst of speed. The Circle N riders gained but little.

A quarter of a mile from the house, Paxton fired one shot in the air. He saw Rooker come charging over the hill from the north. He arrived at the house at the same time that Paxton did. They hit the ground together and raced into the house. Gary was waiting, and Horn had a gun in his hand.

"Indians?" Gary asked.

"Worse," Rooker grunted. "White Indians wearing a Circle N brand."

"If they find out we have inherited this land," Paxton said to Gary, "they'll kill us or die trying. They hired Joshua and Roy killed because they claimed this land."

"They already suspect you're going to inherit the land," Horn said. "They've got a lawyer trying to get legal claim to the land, but he can't make a move until Joshua's will is settled. I made sure of that."

"Then they'll get rid of us any way they can," Paxton said.

"That must be why Kucek was after you," Gary said. "He was being paid to do it."

"I don't doubt it," Paxton agreed. "Now they'll try to wipe us out while they've got us bottled up here." He looked at Horn. "This is hardly the place for a lawyer."

"I figured on a fight when I came," Horn said, staring out the window. "I've got my reasons for being here."

Paxton looked out at the Circle N riders dismounting beyond the corral. He would have asked Horn what his reasons were, but someone out there sent a rifle bullet through a window just then. Paxton forgot about Horn as he concentrated on the Circle N men. It appeared every one had a rifle, and there wasn't a rifle in the house.

Paxton didn't have one, and Rooker had left his on his saddle. A revolver would be of little use at this range.

"Better come out," Norrid shouted from the corral. "There are Indians all around. We could fight them off together."

"The old fool must think we're crazy," Rooker said. "First he shoots at us, then he wants us to come out and join him in fighting Indians."

"The Indians are gone anyway, and he knows it," Paxton said.

"They'll come and burn you out," Norrid yelled.

Paxton saw the doubt in Gary's face. "The Indians won't be back," he said. "Watch that back door. Norrid may send some men around there."

"He'll try to smoke us out," Horn said as Gary moved across the room to the back door.

"This is a perfect setup for Norrid," Paxton said after a pause. "Everybody knows the Indians have raided through this country. What happened to Yount is proof of that. If Norrid and his outfit can kill us and burn the house, who can say the Indians didn't do it?"

"He sure won't let you get away if he can

help it," Rooker said. "He won't want to leave any witnesses either."

"Too bad you're trapped here with us," Gary said.

Rooker shrugged. "Norrid wants me out of the way too. He just hasn't had the chance or the excuse for doing it. Now he has."

"We're not dead yet," Paxton said. "Let's get set for them."

Suddenly, rifles opened up at half a dozen points in the perimeter facing the house. Norrid was beginning his assault.

"Don't fire till you see something you can hit," Paxton warned. "See anything back there, Gary?"

"Nothing here," Gary reported.

The rifles kept barking at intervals. Paxton found some boxes that the Indians had emptied on the floor. He pushed the boxes into the broken windows, giving the attackers less open area through which to see the interior of the house.

"Ortis is out there," Rooker said, pointing. "He's itching for a good shot at us. Wish we had some rifles instead of just revolvers."

"They'll figure out pretty soon that we don't have rifles," Paxton said. "Then they'll get closer."

"Hey, Paxton," Ortis yelled from the corner of the corral. "Why don't you come out and fight me? If you win, everybody else will leave."

"What if you win?" Paxton yelled back.

"The fight will still be over. It's you we want."

Rooker shook his head. "Don't fall for that. They want all of us dead. If they can get rid of you, they know they can handle the rest of us. None of us are gunfighters. I wouldn't trust Ortis as far as I could throw a bull by the tail with one hand."

Paxton watched the activity out by the corral while he thought about it. It might be a trick; Ortis might be faster with a gun than anyone thought. Still, if there was a chance that they could settle this whole thing with a single fight between him and Ortis, it would be worth the try. He'd rather face Ortis alone than to take the chance that they would all be burned in the house.

"Makes sense to me," Paxton said finally.

"Hold on now," Rooker said sharply. "You didn't hear me right. I said I wouldn't trust Ortis."

"Do you trust Norrid not to roast us alive after dark when we can't see them sneak up here?"

"I wouldn't trust him any further than I would Ortis. I don't trust any of that bunch out there."

"Will it be a fair fight?" Paxton yelled.

"Sure," Ortis yelled back. "Just you and me. Everybody here will pull back but me. You come out, and we'll meet in the yard. Whichever way it goes, the fight is over. Everybody else goes home."

"When?" Paxton yelled.

"Half an hour," Ortis yelled back.

"They can think up all kinds of devilment in half an hour," Rooker said.

"They can wait till dark and burn us all too."

"I don't like it," Rooker said. "He knows you killed Kucek this morning. He's not the gunslinger that Kucek was. Why is he willing to face you now?"

"Maybe he thinks he is better than Kucek was. Most gunfighters think they are the best in the world. If I can beat him, we'll have one less to fight out there."

Paxton suspected a trick, yet he had to take the chance that he could spot it and overcome it. He checked his gun carefully. It was ready. The time ticked slowly by. Jeff Rooker said no more. A few minutes before the half hour had run out, Norrid and the rest of the Circle N men backed off a couple of hundred yards.

"They're doing what they said," Rooker muttered. "That doesn't sound like Norrid. Watch those rifles out there, Dave. If they try to use them, we'll do what we can to cover you, but they're out of our range."

"Better than all of us roasting," Paxton said.

His watch showed that the half hour was up. He moved to the door and opened it. Cautiously, he stepped outside. He saw Vic Ortis on the far side of the corral. He wondered if Ortis would have a rifle or shotgun, but he came around the corner of the corral without either, his hand poised above his holstered gun. Everything look right. Still, Paxton was suspicious. Ortis was too confident.

They came within range, and as Paxton moved farther into the yard, he wondered if he was exposing his back to a hidden marksman. He stopped, challenging Ortis to draw. Then suddenly his planning was shattered by the sharp crack of a rifle. He dropped like a rock, but no bullet came near him. He saw Ortis whip his head to the knoll to Paxton's right. Paxton looked that way too. Two men had suddenly leaped up, dropping their rifles and sprinting for the Circle N men who were far back from the fighting. A little puff of smoke up on another ridge showed where the rifle shot had come from.

Paxton came to his feet, furious at the trickery. He had been expecting a trick, but he hadn't located it. He had just moved into sight of the two riflemen.

"Any more tricks, Ortis?" he demanded.

Ortis, his trap exposed, dug for his gun. He was no match for the speed or the accuracy of Paxton. It was all over in a second. As Ortis went down, Paxton shot a glance at the men back in Norrid's group. He saw a couple of rifles being jerked up to point at him. He turned and sprinted, zigzag, for the house. Bullets kicked up dust, but the distance was too far for accurate shooting and Paxton offered an elusive target.

Diving through the door, he landed rolling while Rooker slammed the door shut.

"I told you they'd pull some trick," Rooker yelled.

"Ortis won't pull any more tricks," Paxton said, getting up and rubbing an elbow he had bumped on the floor.

Rooker's face relaxed. "Maybe they'll

believe you're a real ghost now. They can't kill you."

"They'll keep trying," Paxton said.

Several shots were fired into the cabin as Norrid brought the Circle N men back to the corrals, but no rush was made. They were waiting for dark, Paxton guessed. He hadn't gained much except to eliminate their best gun.

As the sun disappeared, Paxton considered trying to sneak out the back way. Suddenly, Gary whispered that someone was coming toward the back door.

"Shoot!" Rooker hissed.

"It looks like a woman," Gary said.

Paxton was across the room in two leaps. Glancing out the window, he saw that it was Loanda. He pushed the back door open and Loanda slipped through.

"I was afraid the Indians had you," he said in relief.

"I was at the Circle N when they went past," she said. "Mr. Norrid was there too. Some riders came in. Said they'd seen you coming this way. Mr. Norrid ordered every man to ride with him. They planned to kill you and blame it on the Indians. I followed them over here. I saw those two men hide out where they could see the yard. I didn't know what was up till you came out to face Vic. That's when I took a hand."

Paxton looked at her with a new feeling he hadn't taken time to analyze before, "Why did you do it?"

She met his gaze directly. "If you don't know, then I made a mistake."

He nodded. "I reckon I know. I hope it's no mistake. We'll get out of this." He looked out the front. "If I had my white coat, hat and horse, I could scare most of those men away."

A sparkle came into Rooker's eyes. "You sure could. By now, most of them just have to believe you're a ghost."

"Nothing white here," Gary said.

"There might be," Loanda said, "if the Indians didn't take it all."

She went to a trunk along the wall and came back in a minute with two long white petticoats.

"Can't make much of a hat out of this, but I can make something that will cover your head. I can split one of these and make a long cape for you. You'll have to do without a white horse."

In five minutes, Loanda was fitting a white cloth over Paxton's head and draping a split petticoat over his shoulders, leaving his gun hand free.

"Going out there will be mighty risky," Gary said.

"Staying here and getting roasted is a little risky too," Paxton said.

Paxton watched Norrid's men. He expected them to surround the house before they tried to set it afire. They wouldn't let anyone escape. But they were still clustered behind the corral close to their horses. The ground behind the house sloped upward, and no one could sneak out the back door and escape without the men at the corral seeing him. They could easily run him down on horseback. When it got dark, it would be different. They'd move around where they could stop anyone who came out the back door.

Paxton waited until it was deep twilight, then slipped out the back door and moved to the corner of the house. There, he tapped the side of the house before moving out into view of the men at the corral. Inside, Rooker and Gary repeated the moans and groans that they had used at Norrid's place in Monotony the night before.

Paxton knew it wasn't likely that every man in the Circle N crew would be afraid of the ghost. But if some of them were, those few would run. That would thin their ranks, and the confidence of those who stayed would surely be shaken.

He was a third of the way to the corral when two shots were fired at him. Both missed, and Paxton held his steady pace. Then the first man broke and ran. The rest went like a tide breaking through a sand barrier. Norrid turned away from Paxton and screamed at the men to come back. They ignored him. One did turn and yell back at Norrid.

"If you're so brave, you shoot him."

Norrid swore at the running men, then wheeled back and started shooting wildly at Paxton. The first shots were far over Paxton's head, and he fought down his panic and kept walking. After the third shot, Norrid paused and Paxton said just loud enough for him to hear, "You can't kill a ghost."

Norrid fired twice more, wilder than ever. Then he threw down his gun and started to run. Paxton fired then, the bullet spurting up the dust just in front of Norrid.

"Stop right there, Norrid!"

Norrid stopped as if he'd hit a stone wall.

Paxton halted, not wanting to get near enough that Norrid could recognize him.

"You have a choice, Elias Norrid," he

said in what he hoped sounded like a ghostly voice. "You let Paxton and Gary Wirth alone or the next time I visit you, you'll die. Is that clear?"

"Clear, clear," Norrid babbled.

"Go," Paxton said, "and don't ever come back to this spring again."

Norrid tried to run to his horse, but he stumbled with almost every step. When he reached the horse, he mounted and charged after his men who were just going out of sight.

Loanda led Rooker and Gary out of the house. Horn stayed behind, too weak to follow. She ran to Paxton, and he caught her in his arms. She gave him a kiss, and he looked over at his brother and Rooker.

"They might as well get used to it," Loanda said. "They're going to see it often if they stay around us."

"We'll check the horses to see if any got hit," Rooker said and led Gary toward the horses near the corner of the house.

Loanda led Paxton toward the house. "I've got a squeaky board in my floor I want you to fix," she said.

He frowned. What a time to think of a squeaky floor board! But he followed her inside. He'd have to tell her that he and

Gary owned this place now. That wasn't going to be easy.

"Norrid doesn't own this land, you know," he said as they stepped inside.

"I know. Nobody knows who will own it till Joshua Greer's will is settled. Mr. Norrid doesn't ever want it to be settled."

"It is settled," Paxton said. "Gary and I have inherited it. But it's your home," he added quickly, "and I want it to stay that way."

"You mean you'll share it with me?"

"Wouldn't have it any other way. Maybe we can buy out Gary's half."

"There's plenty of room on this place for two houses if he wants to build one. I don't intend to give up this house — or you."

"Is that why you want the squeaky board fixed?"

"Isn't that a good reason?" she asked. She stepped on a board near the corner and it squealed. "It isn't nailed down. Look under it."

He stooped and lifted the short board. The nails had been pulled. A tin box was there. He lifted the small box, realizing that it was this box that Loanda had wanted him to look at, not the squeaky board. Before he opened it, he guessed what he was going to find. Joshua had found the buried money and had moved it inside his house.

Loanda had lit the lamp and now she set it on the table near the corner where Paxton was looking in the box.

"This is Joshua's box, all right," Paxton said.

"You're rich now," Loanda said.

"Not very," Paxton said. "This goes to the Union Pacific. It was stolen from them. There is a nice reward for its recovery. You get that. You found it."

"There isn't going to be any reward."

Paxton wheeled toward Mark Horn. He had completely forgotten about the lawyer who had sat back during the fighting and hadn't moved since the excitement had died down. Paxton saw the gun in his hand.

"You're taking it?" Paxton asked in disbelief.

"Half of it," Horn said, "unless you get stubborn. I'm honest in my dealings. Joshua and I were good friends. I handled his legal affairs, and he promised me a split of the money if he found it. So I'll take my half. You can have the rest."

Paxton stared at the lawyer. "That old newspaper clipping Joshua had said that three of the train robbers escaped. Uncle Josh, Kucek, and you. Right?"

Horn stared back at Paxton. Finally he sighed. "Josh and I would have been rich and we'd have had a high time."

"Why did you help Gary and me get this land?" Paxton demanded.

"I didn't want the land, and Josh wanted you to have it. Now you've got it. So give me my share of the money."

"It isn't yours. It goes back to the railroad."

"If you're going to be bull-headed about it, I'll just take Josh's share too," Horn said. "Now back off from that box."

"Lay the gun on the table," Gary said sharply from the front door.

"Easy like," Rooker added from the back door.

Horn hesitated, then seeing two guns pointed at him, moved to the table and laid the gun down. Gary and Rooker came inside. They moved over to look at the box Paxton had taken from under the floor.

Horn sidled toward the door. Paxton saw him, started to touch his gun, then thought better of it. Horn had been through enough. The money was going back. Maybe the books could be closed.

A horse broke into a gallop outside. Rooker jerked his head up. "You know what, Gary? We let our prisoner get away."

"We'll never make good lawmen," Gary said. "But we can see that the money is returned."

"Maybe you two had better see if Horn took all our horses or just his own," Paxton said.

"Just one horse —" Rooker started to say. Then his face broke into a wide grin. "Sure, we'll check. Better watch him, miss," he said to Loanda as he and Gary headed for the front door. "Most people think he is a ghost, but he sure ain't acting like a ghost now."

When they were gone, Paxton reached for Loanda who came to him willingly. "What's your pa going to say?"

"About what?" she asked innocently, hazel eyes wide.

He kissed her, and she snuggled to him. "About you becoming Mrs. Dave Paxton."

"If he says anything, I'll sic the ghost on him," she murmured softly. "Kiss me again. I need to be convinced that you're not a ghost."